"So What Was Your Scenario? That I Was Here To Extort You And Once You Gave Me A Mind-Blowing Send-Off, I'd Walk Away?"

"What else could I think? You can't be considering taking Dora for real," Naomi cried. "For God's sake, Andreas, you know you don't want a baby and won't be able to give her the home and family life she needs and deserves."

He shrugged. "Probably. That's why I don't intend to take Dorothea from you."

Her heart detonated with brutal hope. "Y-you don't?"

Leaning one knee down, he dipped the mattress, tumbling her toward him, and murmured, "I don't."

Before she collapsed back with relief, his hand dove beneath the sheets and cupped her breast, giving it a delicious squeeze. "I do intend to take you, though."

The Sarantos
Baby Bargain

OLIVIA GATES

MILLS & BOON®

First published in Great Britain 2014
by Mills & Boon, an imprint of Harlequin (UK) Limited,
Large Print edition 2014
Eton House, 18-24 Paradise Road,
Richmond, Surrey, TW9 1SR

ISBN: 978 0 263 24428 1

Harlequin (UK) Limited's policy is to use papers that are natural, renewable and recyclable products and made from wood grown in sustainable forests. The logging and manufacturing processes conform to the legal environmental regulations of the country of origin.

Printed and bound in Great Britain
by CPI Antony Rowe, Chippenham, Wiltshire

OLIVIA GATES

has always pursued creative passions such as singing and handicrafts. She still does, but only one of her passions grew gratifying enough, consuming enough, to become an ongoing career—writing.

She is most fulfilled when she is creating worlds and conflicts for her characters, then exploring and untangling them bit by bit, sharing her protagonists' every heart-wrenching heartache and hope, their every heart-pounding doubt and trial, until she leads them to an indisputably earned and gloriously satisfying happy ending.

When she's not writing, she is a doctor, a wife to her own alpha male and a mother to one brilliant girl and one demanding Angora cat. Visit Olivia at www.oliviagates.com

To all my readers. Thanks so much for all your support and enthusiasm. It's for you that I keep writing.

One

Naomi Sinclair stared at the face filling the TV screen in her partner's office, an avalanche of memories swamping her. Memories of a time when she'd known exactly how the *Titanic* had felt.

She'd crashed into her own iceberg, after all. A colossal one by the name of Andreas Sarantos. The one whose ice now reached out from the screen to freeze her marrow…and simultaneously spill lava into her bloodstream.

Despite all the cautionary tales of what befell those who approached him, she'd steamed ahead on an intercept course. When she'd collided with him, it hadn't been for a catastrophic but brief encounter. Oh, no. She'd smashed herself against his frozen annihilation for two tumultuous years. Total wreckage had been the only possible outcome.

Now her whole being quivered at seeing Andreas again, after four long years. With the sound off, and with him looking right at her so fiercely, she could imagine him saying what he'd said that first day she'd pursued him.

You don't want to get mixed up with me, Ms. Sinclair. Walk away. While you still can.

She could still hear his voice, dark and pulsing with sensual menace, that slight Greek accent making it more compelling. Could still feel his eyes burning her with their inimitable brand of aloof yet searing lust.

She hadn't heeded his warning. Not before she'd had a protracted demonstration of how right he'd been. His words had not been a cautioning, but a promise. Of destruction. One he'd carried out. And she'd had no one to blame but herself.

"What do you know! He's back in town."

The comment, laced with surprise and not a little excitement, pulled Naomi back to reality with a thud.

Tearing her gaze from the gorgeous yet forbidding face still filling the screen, she blinked at her partner.

Malcolm Ulrich's comment made her realize where Andreas was. In front of his Fifth Avenue headquarters. He *was* "back in town." Where he hadn't been for four years.

Though she knew he could be in the next room and make no effort to see her, her heart hammered at the realization.

Malcolm turned his gaze to her, his green eyes eager. "I'd just about given up on doing business with him, since he deals only in person, and only when he's here." Her partner looked at the TV again. "But here he is."

She unwillingly followed suit, found Andreas's eyes drilling into hers as he glowered at the camera with all the tolerance of a wolf regarding a rabbit.

Malcolm sighed. "I still can't believe I didn't manage to pin him down to something when he pulled our fat out of the fire back in Crete, then came here personally to discuss how he resolved our problem with Stephanides. But it's never too late, and that guy is bigger than ever. This time I'll do whatever it takes to nail down his elusive hide long enough for him to give our expansion plans serious consideration."

A scoff almost escaped her. She hadn't gotten "serious consideration" from Andreas when she'd been in his bed every night. Not even mind-blowing sex had swayed him to get involved in something he hadn't considered "financially feasible." He'd said their sustainable development methods posed too many logistical problems and promised too little profit for him to bother with. That had been the sum total of the business talk they'd had during their...liaison.

But she doubted telling Malcolm that would dissuade him from continuing his pursuit of Andreas. And it might make him suspect there'd been more between her and Andreas than he, and the world, knew. Only Nadine, her only sister, and Petros, his only friend, had known the truth. To the world, she and Andreas had been two professionals who'd crossed paths sporadically, he as the Greek multi-billionaire venture capitalist whose magic touch every business in the world craved, and she as a partner in a real estate development company struggling to make its mark in an increasingly competitive field.

When it had been over, she'd been endlessly grateful for that fact. No one knew of her folly, making it possible for her to pretend the ordeal had never happened. And she wanted to keep it that way. As much as it pained her, she had to let

Malcolm butt his head against the wall that was Andreas Sarantos.

But it wasn't as if Malcolm didn't know it was probably futile, anyway. He'd been after Andreas's transformative financing even before they'd become partners seven years ago. It was when Andreas finally answered one of Malcolm's persistent invitations that she'd first met him, a year after she, Malcolm and Ken had set up Sinclair, Ulrich & Newman, or SUN Developments.

Andreas had come to inspect one of their first projects, with Malcolm hoping to tempt him to finance their ambitious offshore expansion plans.

From photos, Naomi had already thought him the most incredible looking man she'd ever seen. But it had taken that face-to-face encounter to turn her inside out.

His gaze and handshake had been cool, detached, yet an all-out invasion at the same time. Throughout his fifteen-minute presence, he'd fascinated and intimidated her as no one had ever done. He'd made few comments, but those had been so ruthlessly denuding, they'd uncovered weaknesses neither she nor her partners had realized had been inherent in their system. Then he'd abruptly taken his leave, giving no indication if he'd been interested or not in their business plan—or in her.

That hadn't stopped her from thinking of him to distraction afterward....

The images on the screen changed, interrupting her reminiscing. Her gaze clung to his figure as he strode away to his limo. Even from the back, he looked every inch the indifferent raider who conquered without trying, devastated without effort and cared nothing about the damage he left in his wake. The reporter, a woman evidently unnerved by her close encounter with the Greek god, regretted that she hadn't been able to get enough from Mr. Sarantos.

Enough from, or of? a voice inside Naomi scoffed.

But if she could have given the woman a word of advice, she would have told her that no one got a thing from Andreas Sarantos. Nothing but hurt, heartache and humiliation.

Malcolm reached for his cell phone. "I'd better call him right away, reserve the first free hour he has while he's here, before the whole city starts hounding him."

Feeling as if she'd run a mile, Naomi rose unsteadily to her feet. "I'll leave you to it."

"Hey..." Malcolm stood, too, his expression dismayed. "We haven't even started our meeting."

"There's always tomorrow." Naomi stopped at

the door, mainly to lean on it until she regained her balance. "And I'd probably be useless to you, worrying about Dora, anyway."

Which was, incidentally, true. Leaving Dora with a slight fever had made her unable to focus on anything all day. She'd spent most of it checking back with Hannah obsessively, though her nanny kept insisting everything was fine. Now Andreas's unexpected return—even when Naomi was certain that the news spot would be her only exposure to him—had finished off any possibility for coherent thinking today. Might as well head home early.

She attempted a smile. "Just as well you found a more important thing to pursue today."

"Nothing is more important than you!"

Naomi's smile remained unchanged at his protest, and she made no response as she closed his office door behind her.

Malcolm had always made such gallant statements, but lately she'd been detecting something more in his courteous remarks. Something she hoped she was wrong about. She'd hate it if anything spoiled their friction-free working relationship and friendship. She'd started the partnership with him and Ken in the first place because both men had been happily married. But after Malcolm's wife died from cancer three years ago, she'd started picking up different vibes from him. They'd become more noticeable since Nadine's and Petros's deaths three months ago. Naomi dreaded thinking Malcolm might be rebooting his program with her as the object of his monogamy.

Her mind was overflowing with this disturbing possibility and with Andreas's out-of-the-blue return when she entered her apartment in Manhattan's Upper East Side.

She'd thrown her purse on the foyer table and was hastily hanging up her coat when she heard footsteps rushing toward her. She swung around to find Hannah, once her nanny and now Dora's, looking anxious.

The heart that had been thudding all the way here now pounded with alarm. "Is Dora's fever up again? Why didn't you call me? I would have come back at once, taken her to the doctor!"

Hannah looked momentarily taken aback before waving her hand. "Oh, I told you countless times today that her temperature went down after you gave her medicine, and hasn't come up again. We had a wonderful day and she went down for the night a couple of hours early."

Naomi leaned against the wall as tension deflated abruptly. She exhaled. "When you came rushing like that—God, my mind's been all over the place, more than usual today."

Sympathy overflowed in Hannah's shrewd hazel eyes. "After what you've been through, it's natural for you to be jumpy. It's amazing you've held up this well. But you don't have to worry about Dora. Robust little tykes like her can weather far more than a temperature. After raising four kids of my own, and you and Nadine, with Dora my seventh baby, I should know."

"While I feel I know nothing," Naomi lamented. "Next week Dora will be ten months old and I still feel like a total novice. I keep worrying every minute she's out of my sight. Accidents do happen…." Like the accident that had taken Nadine's and Petros's lives.

The words clogged in her throat, the wound that had never stopped bleeding for the past three months opening yet again.

Hannah reached for her, gave her one of those hugs that, as far back as she could remember, had always made things better even at the worst of times. "Being paranoid is part of being a parent, sweetie. And you have more reason than usual for your anxieties. But we won't let anything happen to our Dora, ever, and she'll grow up safe and loved, and become a beautiful, exceptional woman like her mom and aunt."

Agony swelled all over again as her sister's exuberant face filled Naomi's mind. Before tears flowed, she nodded into Hannah's ample shoulder, letting her touch and scent soothe her. Hannah had always been an integral part of her life, filling the void her mother had left behind when she'd died when Naomi was only thirteen.

Sniffling and attempting a smile, she pulled away. "So why did you come rushing to the door like that? Did you think I was an intruder or something, since I'm a bit early? Shouldn't you have come armed?" Her smile wobbled as another alarm sent her hair-trigger nerves into an uproar again. "If you ever suspect anything of the sort, lock yourself in a room with Dora and call the police—"

Hannah raised both hands. "You really *are* extra jumpy today. This apartment building is intruder-proof, and you've certainly padlocked all entrances against an invading army. Anyone who comes in here has to be invited." She stopped, hesitated, unease creeping over her genial face again. "Which brings me to the reason I rushed out to intercept you."

"Intercept me…before what?"

"Before you walked into your family room and found *me*."

Naomi lurched, a spear of shock lodging in her heart.

That voice. The voice that had never stopped whispering its insidious spell inside her mind.

Andreas.

A bolt of stupefaction wrenched her around.

And there he was, filling the archway of her foyer.

Andreas Sarantos. The man she'd barely escaped four years ago, with her soul and psyche in tatters.

It was impossible, preposterous for him to be here. In her apartment, where he'd never even dropped her off, let alone set foot inside, during the years they'd been together…though not really together.

But there he was. His presence reached out and enveloped her, drowned her. Elemental, primal. Bigger than she remembered, broader, more ominous. He stared at her across the dozen feet of barely breathable air that was all that stood between them. Then he started obliterating them.

He approached like advancing darkness, and his aura eclipsed her, made her insides quiver with a mess of reactions she'd never thought she'd experience again. If anything, time had faded her memories of his impact. Or had he grown more overwhelming?

But he can't be here, her mind screamed, as her heartbeats spiraled into the danger zone.

The chips of steel he had for eyes captured hers, freezing her to the spot. Then they swept her from head to toe, engulfing her in simmering ice.

Her gaze careered down his body in return. From sun-gilded hair, to skin the texture and color of polished teak, to the slashes and planes and hollows of a face assembled with ruthless perfection. His body was shrouded in a suit that looked molded on him. She knew from extensive experience that the flesh beneath had been carved by a divine hand. But all that physical flawlessness would have never affected her if it hadn't been imbued with a charisma and character that bent masses to his merest whim. This man, this force of darkness, commanded thousands, his every decision and action impacting millions. And he'd once had her completely in his power, to do with as he pleased. As she'd once begged him to.

She'd also once begged him to let her go. Because even then she'd feared she wouldn't have the strength to walk away. What he'd done next, to spite her, to torment her, had had her swearing *never again.*

But she'd believed she had nothing to worry about. That he'd disappeared from her life forever. After his latest and most terrible transgression, she'd been certain she would never lay eyes on him again.

But there he was. Why? *Why?*

"What the hell are you doing here?"

She barely recognized the alien rasp that hissed out of her. Then she heard Hannah's agitated voice.

"When I found him at the door, I assumed you instructed the concierge to send him up. And since you do know him, I let him in." Even Hannah thought the extent of Naomi's acquaintance with Andreas had merely been a few encounters when her sister had married his friend. "He led me to believe you *did* invite him, said he had to arrive early, but insisted I didn't disturb you at work, and that he'd wait for you."

Naomi turned to Hannah, barely processing her apologetic account, only one thing registering within the mass of shock her brain had become. Fury.

Before she could assure her the fault had all been Andreas's, he spoke again, addressing the older woman. "Thank you for being the perfect hostess, Mrs. McCarthy. Tea was lovely. But now that Naomi is here, you can tend to your other business."

He was dismissing her!

And Hannah, one of the strongest characters Naomi had ever known, was already obeying him without hesitation, not even pausing to catch her eye to check if that was okay with her.

This tipped her still reverberating shock over the edge into pure outrage.

She ground her teeth as she turned to him, pulling herself to her full height, even though it still left her almost a foot shorter than his six foot five. "Now that I am here, *you* can go."

Andreas waited until Hannah disappeared, no doubt to the farthest recess of the apartment, then cocked his head at Naomi. "I will go…back to your family room. Or would you prefer we conduct this meeting in some other room?"

Some other room.

His words dripped with nuance. Not that he necessarily meant the bedroom. He'd once turned every square foot of wherever they'd met into a setting for intimacy. The sexual variety only, of course.

That he could imply any such thing now added another layer of blackness to his already dark-assin character.

"The only place you'll go is out," she gritted. "Whatever you're here for, it's way too late. Everything—*everyone*—is long dead and buried."

The Andreas she once knew would have met her rebuke with nothing but blankness in his eyes. The one actual reaction she'd seen, apart from incinerating passion, had been the last time they'd been together. He'd shocked her with his anger then. It had infuriated him that she'd mustered the will to end whatever it was between them. She'd been his handy outlet and it had enraged him that she'd been the one to end it all, probably only before he'd been ready with a replacement.

But now she could read some response in his gaze. Within the unfathomable steel-gray of his eyes, there was the stirring of surprise, of calculation, of...amusement?

He found death and burials amusing? Probably. He must also be marveling at the puny human who dared defy the god that he was. If so, she'd give him some serious entertainment.

Turning on her heel, only rage holding her together, Naomi reached for her purse and phone. She punched three numbers.

With a finger hovering over the call button, she turned to him. "Get out right now, or I'm contacting the police and reporting that you conned your way in here, and are staying against my will."

Looking totally unconcerned by her threat, he calmly said, "Once you hear why I'm here, you'll beg me to stay."

"I'd sooner beg a shark to devour me."

Those lethal lips twisted so offhandedly that frustration expanded inside her. "Speaking of devouring… The last time I ate was that horrid meal on my flight here."

"Whatever happened? Have you now joined mere mortals in suffering commercial flights?"

He gave a shrug of dismissal, since of course multibillionaire Andreas Sarantos had his own fleet of jets.

"Even food on private jets can be bad. At least it seemed that way as I sat for the past thirty minutes being tormented by Mrs. McCarthy's mouthwatering cooking aromas. I bet she made enough to accommodate my presence. Let's honor her efforts and have this conversation over dinner."

Naomi shook her head, as if that might make this nightmare fade away. But it was really happening. He truly was here, disregarding her anger and threats, and inviting himself to dinner. It was so atrociously arrogant, it numbed her.

She shook her head again. "I know you believe

everyone is a chess piece in the game you perpetually play. But if you think you can still move me around, you've progressed from being detached from humanity to detached from reality."

He met her low-voiced tirade with a cool-eyed stare. She snapped her fingers in front of his face. "See this? I really exist and I'm done playing my role in an act where you have the only lines. Now for the last time—get out."

She could almost see her wrath shattering against the indifference he wore like impenetrable armor. If a fallen angel did exist, he had to look and feel exactly like Andreas. Terribly beautiful, sinister and sublime at once, impossible to withstand or to look away from.

He tilted his head, causing his now collar-length hair to sift to the side with a sigh. She suppressed a shudder at the sound, her hands fisting at the memory of threading through those layers of silk.

Then he tsked in mock reproach. "After four years of separation, is this any way to talk to your beloved husband?"

Two

Husband.

The word—the *lie*—detonated inside Naomi's head.

"*Ex*-husband!"

Her barked qualification had no impact on him whatsoever.

He only shrugged. "Technicality."

His nonchalance as he reduced some of her life's worst times to nothing exacerbated her fury.

"That 'technicality' is called *divorce.*"

And it hadn't been the easy, quick one she'd believed it would be when she'd demanded it. He'd put her through hell before he'd allowed her to conclude the "technicality" that had ended the empty charade they'd called a marriage.

He gave another shrug, even more careless, more provocative. "Why all the drama? Anyone hearing you would think you're a woman scorned, when in fact you were the one who left me."

"This self-centered affliction of yours has reached its terminal stages, hasn't it? You really are incapable of considering anything but your own concerns or anyone but yourself."

"Is there a point you're getting at, or did you just have a bad day and are in need of some venting?"

Her mouth opened, closed. Being a normal human with regular emotions had always caused her severe frustration and disappointment in the face of his total detachment. But this was beyond anything he'd exposed her to. He *had* reached the nirvana of indifference.

He went on. "If you've nurtured some imaginary grievances against me in the years we've been apart, I wouldn't mind standing here until you have your fill of verbal abuse."

"It's only abuse if it isn't true. And I don't have vocabulary enough to describe the awfulness of your truth."

"I don't have any experience with the practice, but I hear some people find bashing others very cathartic."

She finally realized how "some people" had apoplectic fits. "That's it. I won't tolerate your presence a minute longer."

"You mean that up till now that was you being tolerant?"

"Get. Out. Andreas."

He leveled those arctic eyes on hers for fraught moments, until she felt he'd given her a cold burn. Then he turned on his heel…and headed inside.

She stared at his receding figure until he disappeared. Then she was flying after him, with nothing left in her but the need to stop him from invading her life again.

Her fingers turned into talons as they sank into his arm. It was so thick, so hard she had to grab it with both hands and wrench with her full strength. That still didn't make him turn around. She bet he finally stopped of his own accord. He was showing her how she had no effect on him and no say in his actions or decisions. As if she didn't already know that.

Another wave of fury crashed within her when he turned in utmost tranquility. That snapped her last viable nerve.

She hit him. With both fists. Pounded on his formidable chest with all the bitterness that had long been bottled up inside her. Struck him again and again.

He just stood there, bearing her aggression without a change of expression, letting her "vent," watching her intently, as if documenting the reactions of a strange and unstable entity. His lack of reaction cracked her open, had every loss and grief she'd ever suffered spewing out, swamping her in agony now that the leash of control had snapped.

Then suddenly, both hands were behind her back, held in the shackle of one of his, and she was pressed between the cold wall and his hot body. Before she could snatch in another ragged breath, one of his knees drove between her legs, splaying them, his other hand at her nape, tangling in her hair, securing her head, completing her imprisonment.

After one last glance into her eyes, a declaration of intent that had her choking on déjà vu, he bore down on her and crushed his lips to hers. And poisonous memories flooded her, plunging her into the past.

It had been exactly like this, when she'd gone to his hotel suite that first time, demanding he take her up on her insistent offer of herself. She'd instinctively known the edge of roughness was integral to his nature. But she'd felt he'd pushed the envelope, trying to scare her away. When that didn't work, sending her wild with desire instead, he'd pushed some more, testing how much she would allow.

She'd allowed him everything, had reveled in the unbridled power of his passion. From that first night, he'd given her physical pleasure beyond imagining. He'd mined her body for responses and ecstasies she hadn't known it capable of. With every encounter, he'd escalated the wildness of his possession and the ferocity of her satisfaction. But without the development of any emotional response on his part, even intense sexual gratification had started leaving her feeling drained, used up, like an addict who experienced indescribable highs, followed by crashes to dismal depths.

His conquering rumbles filled her now as he angled his hard lips against hers for a deeper invasion. He plucked at her trembling flesh with his teeth, plunged into her recesses, his tongue a slide of sex and silk against hers, inundating her in sensations, each acutely remembered and longed for.

Her surrender, even if it was with shock, not willingness as it had been before, made him take his sensual assault to the next level. His hand twisted in a fistful of her hair, sending a thousand arrows of pleasure to her core. Then he ground his arousal into her quivering belly, making that core spasm, then melt.

But it was his growl of enjoyment that caused her legs to buckle. "You taste even more intoxicating than I remember."

And you taste exactly as I remember. Overwhelming...indispensable...

No. She'd already fallen into that abyss. Twice. *Never again.*

Feeling as if she was being dragged under, drowning, she tried to squirm out of his hold, fighting not only his hunger, but hers, too. She only managed to grind herself harder into his potency. Her only hope of escape would be if he decided to let her go.

He only eased his grip by degrees, dragged his lips from her gasping mouth and across her cheek, nipping her earlobe on the way to her throat. For heart-thundering moments he sucked at her pulse point, as if he wanted to draw her heartbeats out of her. Then with a final groan, he set her hands free and raised his head.

He didn't step away, kept their bodies fused. She remained still, not even breathing as that only pressed her closer to him. Not that she could move. It was all she could do to contain the tremors that threatened to shake her apart. It was his body's support that kept her upright. And it was he who finally backed away from her, with such care, as if his flesh had melded to hers and sudden separation would tear off a layer of their skin.

It wasn't far from the truth. Every inch he'd imprinted felt raw, every nerve he'd strummed exposed. His scent and feel still pounded in her core, his brooding eyes leaving her no place to hide, no chance to regain her composure.

Finally he stepped back, putting just a foot of charged space between them. She drew in a tremulous breath, hoping oxygen would kick-start her volition.

"I won't apologize for hitting you," she murmured. "I bet it's the response you were after, so you'd have an excuse to do what you just did. You manipulated me into doing exactly what you want, as you always did. Good for you. Now leave. Or it won't be your chest my next blows target."

His eyes narrowed to steel slits, the flames of lust still flickering in their depths. "I like this new fire. You were always too...accommodating before."

"You mean submissive."

His gaze grew contemplative as he pursed lips fuller in the aftermath of the devouring he'd subjected her to. "Is that how you saw yourself?"

"It was how I was."

"Not from my point of view. But then you made it clear you think I invent my own convenient, totally inaccurate version of reality. But for what it's worth, I thought you were…pliant, yet never truly submissive." His hand suddenly rose to her face, then he lowered it oh so slowly, running the back of his forefinger down her temple, cheek, neck and collarbone before pausing at the top of her cleavage. His voice dipped an octave into the darkest reaches of hypnosis. "You not only found pleasure in submitting to my demands and desires, but you demanded and took what you wanted as well."

Heat surged in her loins with every recollection of those countless times she'd demanded and taken, when he'd let her feast on him until she'd lost herself in the delight.

She shrank back from his touch, which felt as if it had burned a hole right through her. That wouldn't have been enough to sever the contact if he hadn't dropped his hand.

She hated him for being the only one who'd ever been able to toy with her so effortlessly, hated herself more for allowing him to, for being so susceptible to him still.

She forced out a thick whisper. "I don't think you're here to discuss our defunct liaison…."

His slanting eyebrow arched at the word.

"You're right," she continued. "If I could find a word that's more trivial and impersonal than *liaison,* I would have used it. Anyway, I'm not interested in dredging up a past I've left behind, with a person I should have never gotten mixed up with, as you so kindly pointed out to me at the beginning."

He shoved his hands into his pockets, drawing her gaze to his daunting and unabated arousal. It had just been pressed against her flesh, reminding her of all the times it had invaded her, driven her beyond all sense of self and self-preservation with urgency and ecstasy.

She snatched her gaze up, found him watching her with that cool assessment that made her want to scream.

No doubt satisfied that he'd again provoked her, in every way, he half turned. "I am going to sit down. Coming?"

Without waiting, he continued to her family room, as if those explosive minutes that had thrown the precarious stability of her world back into chaos hadn't occurred.

This time she managed not to pursue and attack him. Not because her anger had lessened, but because she knew he'd respond the same way. She couldn't withstand another assault on her senses. Knowing him, he might even take it further, press on until he made her beg him not to stop. Even now she feared he'd make her do whatever he wanted her to.

Feeling as if her legs had turned to soggy sand-bags, she followed him into her family room.

She'd not only childproofed recently, but also redecorated the space, to make it cheery for Dora and to counter the melancholy that permeated her and the place since Nadine's and Petros's deaths. Now Andreas walked into it and his presence made the room darken and shrink, as he'd always done to her whole world.

He headed to the high-backed red armchair beside the gleefully floral L-shaped couch, which he must have occupied as he'd waited for her. The tea tray on the coffee table and the briefcase on the floor affirmed her deduction.

After he'd resumed sitting, he swept back the hair that had fallen over his forehead during their tussle, drawing her aching gaze again to its luxuriousness. If anything, the longer tresses made him appear even more masculine, made every slash and hollow of his face more rugged. Each change in him did. His every line and feature had been honed to a fiercer virility. And she'd thought he'd already been the epitome of manhood.

Damn him.

But that was only a facade. He was as monstrous on the inside as he was divine on the outside.

He cocked his head at her when she remained standing several feet away. "Your reaction to seeing me wasn't spur-of-the-moment. Seems your animosity has been brewing for a long time."

Those statements made her scoff incredulously. "If I didn't know you have a family somewhere, I'd have thought you were grown in a lab, an experiment in producing a frighteningly efficient humanoid devoid of feelings or scruples."

His expression showed no offense, no amusement, no challenge. Nothing at all, as usual. "If this is how you see me, it's your prerogative. But don't you think the impervious entity you describe wouldn't have tried to keep you from leaving him?"

"I think you would do nothing else, to assert

your dominance. You were being a dog in the manger when you refused to finalize the divorce. You never really married me, just signed a bunch of papers to stop me from ending our ill-advised affair, only to continue it under the false label of marriage, on the same barren grounds."

"And I tried to stop you from leaving me, twice, just to 'assert my dominance'? Don't you think it was too much trouble for just that?"

"Not at all. I believe you'd go to any lengths to maintain your record."

That eyebrow arched again. "What record is that?"

"Your perfect one of having everyone at your disposal and everything done according to your rules and at your command."

"Interesting." He scratched the stubble she still felt burning her cheeks, looking as if he was considering a new perspective, before leveling his gaze on her. "That is me to a tee, but none of that was among my motives at the time. I was only trying to wait out your tantrum until you came back to me."

"Tantrum? Is this how you saw it? And if so, what made you decide to let go of the tug-of-war? Did you wake up one day and say to yourself, 'To hell with it, who needs a brat?' It wasn't as if you could have gotten fed up, after all. You weren't even involved in plaguing and pestering me. You just sicced your lawyer on me and went about your business, not once appearing in the picture."

"You must have a theory why I finally let go."

"Probably because even such hassle-free vindictiveness eventually got old."

He made no corroboration of her explanation, nor did he provide his own of why after six months he'd suddenly decided to sign the divorce papers.

Not that she would have accepted any reason he gave. Her analysis made the most sense. He'd gotten bored. Or he'd found a satisfactory replacement. Or many.

"You were right." That made her blink. He was admitting it? But he went on, "I'm not here to recycle past conflicts. But though you claim to have no desire to do that, it seems you're pretty hung up on them."

"My disgust with you has nothing to do with our past."

"What then?"

"You really have no clue, huh?"

"None. Enlighten me."

"Petros called you on his deathbed." The words seethed through gritted teeth. "You didn't bother coming back. You let him die without making the effort to see him one last time. You didn't even attend his funeral."

All the response she got was a slow blink. Then those lasers he had for eyes resumed regarding her with the same steady appraisal, waiting for her to continue.

The emotional bile backed up in her system poured out, swerving from outrage on Petros's behalf to hers. "*Everyone* came. Even business rivals, even *enemies*. Everyone knew Nadine was my world. And that Petros had become the brother I never had. Everyone put everything aside and came or at least called to console me. *You* didn't."

Another slow blink allowed her bitterness to gain momentum, as she finally understood why his absence had hurt so much. "Somehow your disregard made everything that happened between us even worse. I was always ashamed I threw myself at you, blamed myself for everything that happened afterward, but that day I *despised* myself for it, for pursuing, then staying with someone so…warped. When you didn't answer your only friend's dying plea, and didn't grant me even a few empty words of sympathy, I finally realized the magnitude of the crime I'd committed against myself. I never hated anyone in my life. I never hated you even after all you put me through. But when you proved you were worse than a stranger, worse than an enemy…I finally hated you that day."

His lashes lowered again, giving the momentary impression of him being moved, disturbed.

Then he raised his eyes, and they were their usual unfathomable chips of steel. "I didn't realize you'd appreciate seeing or hearing from me at the time."

Her jaw dropped. "Are you pretending you didn't come or call, in deference to my feelings? Play another one."

"I'm stating what I believed. But that wasn't why I didn't come or call."

She waited for him to tell her the reason. A heartbeat later she realized she'd fallen into the trap of expectation all over again. He wouldn't be giving her anything to quench her curiosity or indignation, would never justify his actions or seek understanding or even tolerance for them.

At least she could always count on him for that. No excuses. Everyone invariably lied, or pulled their punches to observe decorum or butter others up, or at least spare their feelings. Not Andreas.

And it would continue to sink in. The magnitude of what she'd risked when she'd thrown herself, body and soul, into his void. Even now he realized she'd been in need of support from any familiar face at the time—he still didn't bother to say he was sorry.

It seemed disappointment and disillusion had no end with Andreas.

Suddenly, she was tired. So very tired. She'd been struggling to act strong, to appear intact, for so long now. First for her mother, then for Nadine, then for Dora and Hannah. But she could no longer pretend she was on Andreas's level, when no one was, and when she was at her most brittle. He was a disturbance she couldn't afford, a battle she couldn't fight. She needed whatever strength she had left for Dora.

All fight gone out of her, she walked to him, no longer minding if he saw how fragile she was, how she was no match for him. "Whatever your reasons for not coming to the funeral, it was for the best, Andreas. Your presence would have only made me feel worse. It's the worst thing you could have done, coming back now. Whatever brought you here, it doesn't matter. Just go. Please."

In response, his hand reached for hers, cradled it in its warmth. Then, with an effortless tug, he had her spilling into his lap, sinking in his power and heat.

Before another neuron fired, a buzz went through her. Seconds stretched out before she realized what it was. His phone.

That galvanized her to push out of his arms. He only tightened them and groaned, "Don't, *omorfiá mou.*"

She shivered at the way his magnificent voice vibrated as he called her "my beauty," just as she always had when a Greek endearment flowed from those spectacular lips.

Keeping her wrapped in one arm, he got his phone out, evidently to silence it, then groaned again when he saw the caller's name.

He dragged in a harsh breath. "I have to take this." He clasped her closer as she squirmed again, immobilizing her with his mesmerizing gaze. "I'm picking up right where I left off afterward."

She somehow managed to rise from his embrace, making it to the couch opposite before collapsing on it. "No, you won't."

His eyes smoldered, running over her with his intention to do just as he'd promised. Then he answered the call, and the name he said...Stephanides. Could it be...?

Next moment he said Christos. So it *was* him. The man who'd once threatened to smash her knee-caps…and worse.

It was how everything had started between her and Andreas, six years ago. She'd been in Crete with Malcolm to set up a branch of their company. They'd been about to close a deal when one day, thugs had accosted them, delivering a threat from Christos Stephanides, *the* local real estate development tycoon. The message had been succinct. Either they took their business elsewhere or they wouldn't leave Crete in one piece.

But before the thugs could give them a taste of what awaited them if they didn't comply, Andreas had materialized out of nowhere and spoken one word: "Leave." The ruffians had almost vanished into thin air in their rush to do just that.

In his usual concise way, Andreas had said he'd deal with the thugs' boss, and had advised them to leave Crete until he told them it was safe to come back. They'd done so, unquestioningly.

Once home, though still shaken, Naomi had been more disappointed. That the one man she'd ever been interested in remained the only man who hadn't tried to approach her.

Nadine had thought his appearance at the moment they'd needed him had to mean something. She'd insisted that next time they met, if he didn't make a move, Naomi should take matters into her own hands.

Having no faith in her sister's romantic notions, Naomi had been surprised and delighted when she'd found Andreas in Malcolm's office days later. He'd seared her in his focus again, but had made no move. And she'd ended up taking Nadine's advice, inviting him to dinner. It was then that Andreas had issued his famous warning, turning her down.

Mortified at his rejection, she'd told Nadine that her advice had backfired. Her sister had still insisted that maybe he'd truly believed it wasn't good for her to know him. Maybe he was being kind, letting her down easy. What had Naomi known about Andreas anyway?

But she'd known what should have been enough. Everybody said he was an iceberg, a man with no feelings, relationships or friendships, who lived only to accumulate more success and money. The presence of females in his life had consisted of abundant one-nights stands.

Not that any of that had discouraged her in the least. She'd still wanted nothing more than to be with him, to appease the unstoppable hunger she'd felt for him, come what may. So she'd approached him again.

This time, Andreas had agreed to her invitation. But as if to test her limits, he'd insisted she come to his hotel suite. Certain that he'd posed no danger beyond the emotional—and she'd had no intention of getting emotionally involved—she'd gone to him.

Bluntly, he'd told her he'd never wanted anything the way he wanted her. But he'd left her alone, knowing she wouldn't be able to withstand him. His ominous words had been blatant with the implication of his insatiability, as well as what she'd realized only later. His total disregard and insensitivity.

But she couldn't blame him for any of that. He'd made his terms brutally clear. If she stayed, he would devour her. But he was nothing she might want in a man. Beyond passion and pleasure, he had nothing to offer her.

Drunk with desire and recklessness, she'd told him that was exactly what she wanted, too. Since her mother had died, she'd taken care of her four-years-younger sister, becoming an adult prematurely. Naomi hadn't made one step since before taking every possible ramification into consideration. Even her professional life was steeped in feasibility studies and risk calculations. But she'd wanted Andreas as she'd never wanted anything else. She couldn't approach that desire with caution.

And starting that night, she'd let him sweep her like a tornado into a tempestuously passionate affair that had been beyond anything she'd dreamed of. Sex between them had been, even according to him, unparalleled, the pleasure escalating and the lust unquenchable.

But soon she'd found her emotions becoming involved—or they had been all along, and she'd lied to herself so that she'd accept his noninvolvement terms. Apart from his inability to feel, Andreas had been everything she could have admired and loved in a man. Brilliant, driven, disciplined, enterprising and a hundred other things that appealed to everything in her. Being a phenomenal lover had ended any hope that her emotions would remain unscathed for long. As he'd made love to her, it had been impossible not to delude herself that his ferocious passion, his meticulous catering to her needs, hadn't been signs of caring. That was, until he'd stepped out of bed and reverted to iceberg mode.

It had taken only four months for the lack of an emotional dimension to make her confess she'd been wrong to think she could handle the terms of their involvement. She couldn't wait for things to deteriorate between them, and it was best to part when they had only the fantastic memories.

In answer, he'd only brooded as she'd walked away, not trying to stop her....

"Christos sends his regards."

Her heart fired as his calm voice yanked her from the past, landing her in the present with a thud.

Her glower was equally for him and for the hoodlum who paraded as a businessman and dared pretend they were on a cordial footing. Though it surprised her Andreas had told him he was with her. He'd never acknowledged her before.

"Tell him I'm sending them back as undeliverable. And when he gets them, he knows where to put them."

Andreas's eyebrows rose slightly, his closest expression to amusement. "He will be shocked a lady like you could be so...harsh. Especially since he's taken such a shine to you."

Yeah, and he had tried to "acquire" her "golden

beauty" as if she were part of their business deal. "The feeling is certainly not mutual."

"That would only make you even more enticing in his eyes. Mere men expect the goddess that you are wouldn't reciprocate their interest, expect you to be haughty and out of reach."

Was he speaking as a fellow god who knew how he affected mere women? Not that she could accuse him of exaggerating when he called her a goddess. He'd always lavished praise on her that had surpassed poetry. It had been what had kept her with him for two years through the alienation on all other fronts. That and the sheer perfection of their chemistry.

He put his phone away. "I now understand the source of your current antipathy toward me. But why is Christos still in the bull's-eye of your wrath? Your conflict has long been resolved."

Strange that he wasn't taking credit for that, when it had been he who'd gotten Stephanides to relent and then to even do business with her company. They'd done a couple of very lucrative projects together before things had fallen through again, if amicably this time. Not that she was about to thank Andreas for that right now, or for anything else.

Gathering what felt like her last spark of energy, she sat forward. "Listen, I'm sure you didn't come here to chat about your money- and image-laundering business buddies, or to exercise your irresistible sexual prowess on me—"

"I didn't intend to touch you…not during this meeting. But it seems nothing has changed. It remains impossible for us to be around each other and not ignite."

His quiet response shuddered through her. That he claimed she affected him as he did her tipped her beyond endurance.

"Enough, Andreas," she groaned. "Whatever you came here for, just spit it out."

He gazed at her in silence until she felt her every cell begin to crackle.

Then, in absolute tranquility, he inclined his head. "As you wish. I'm here to claim Dorothea."

Three

Naomi found herself on her feet, looking down at Andreas. He only tipped his head back as he met her flabbergasted stare, his gaze steady and earnest.

And she exploded. "What kind of *sick* joke is this?"

He rose with the utmost economy and composure, was towering over her before she could take a breath or a step back.

"It isn't a joke. When Petros called me—"

"You didn't come back."

"I didn't need to. He was calling me to—"

"I don't give a damn why he called you, or about anything you're going to say. Dora is mine."

"Dorothea is Petros's."

Naomi's heart pounded until it felt like a wrecking ball inside her chest. "*And* my sister's."

But she'd lost Nadine so recently, the loss so overwhelming and fresh, she hadn't yet started Dora's adoption process. But she'd been sure there was no rush, that her claim to Dora was uncontestable.

She said so. "With Petros being an only child, and with his parents dead, Dora has no other family but me. That makes her *mine*."

"Petros wanted her to be mine."

Naomi shook her head, trying to stop the world that was suddenly spinning, feeling as if he'd punched her square in the face. "God…every time I think I know what depths you can sink to, I discover there's no limit to your callousness. But this…this is a new depth, even for you. This is… evil."

He moved past her, giving her a sideways glance that froze her blood and started it boiling all at once. "As I said, what you think of me is your prerogative. That doesn't change the fact that Petros, Dora's father, wished me to have her."

Afraid she'd keel over if she moved too fast, Naomi turned to face him, found him across the coffee table, both hands back in his pockets, staring at her broodingly.

He wasn't joking. He meant it. This was real.

A hysterical giggle burst out of her.

He only inclined his head in what looked like a nod. "I can understand your shock. I'd hoped I could introduce the subject in a better way, at least gradually. But we couldn't even establish any semblance of a conversation, with you being so hostile and uncooperative."

"Sure, I'm to blame for that. I'm the one who tormented you for six months for laughs, before granting you your freedom. I'm the one who disregarded my dying friend's plea for me to be there for him in his last hours. I'm the one who's standing right there pretending I'm willing to take on a baby, when I made it cuttingly clear I never wanted a child."

"It doesn't matter what I want anymore."

"But it matters what you can or can't do. And I'd sooner believe you'd give birth to a baby rather than take one on."

He had the temerity to huff in what sounded like amusement.

But even if all she wanted was to scratch his eyes out, she had to summon all her diplomacy and end this. This was too…huge for her to let it go any further.

"Listen, Andreas, if you're suffering from belated guilt, for not being there for Petros when he needed you, and you think you should do something for his daughter when you never did a thing for him, don't bother. Petros is dead and gone, and nothing you do or don't do can hurt or help him anymore. If some anomalous sense of duty regarding Dora has been roused inside you, just steer it away until it dies down, as I'm sure it will as soon as this misguided mission is over and you walk out of here. Dora doesn't need your guardianship and is perfectly safe and happy and provided for with me."

"I have no doubt you are an exemplary aunt—"

"I am more than Dora's aunt. *I gave birth to her!*"

At her cry, it was as if all the air was sucked out of the room. Something fierce reverberated from him in shock waves.

He didn't know?

She rushed to explain. "Nadine and Petros wanted a baby so much, but it was impossible for her to get pregnant or to carry her own baby to term. So I became their surrogate for the baby they made together." She'd wanted to help them, and also thought it would be the only way she'd ever have a baby. "Dora is my flesh and blood in *every* way."

"I know."

His quiet words lurched through her.

So what had caused that fierce reaction? Or had she imagined it? Probably. Andreas experienced no such reactions.

He went on. "Not that it makes a difference what you are to her. It's what Petros wanted me to be to her that's the issue here."

Hanging on to control with all she had, she asked, "When did he even make that so-called last wish? Over the phone? In that call you now claim wasn't to ask you to come back before he died?"

"That's what I tried to say when you interrupted me. He didn't ask me to come back for him, but for Dorothea."

"Wow, this keeps getting better. He asked you that three months ago, and you just got around to it now? If Dora had you to count on, she would have been lost somewhere in the system by the time you deemed it convenient to come for her."

"I knew she was safe with you."

"So there was no rush, huh? And there will never

be one, so you can return to wherever you've disappeared for the past four years, and just never come back again."

"I can't and won't do that."

"Don't posture. It was just something Petros said."

"It was something he wrote. In his will."

That felt like a resounding slap across her face.

A minute passed before she stammered, "I—I can't believe Petros wrote such a will. If he did, he must have been panicking after the accident, when he suspected from everyone's evasions that Nadine was dead, and realized he'd die, too." Naomi shook her head. "And it still doesn't make sense he'd think you'd make Dora a better guardian than me."

"He didn't ask for me to be her guardian. He wanted me to give her my name."

She gaped at him. He looked deadly serious. And she found herself staggering back and collapsing on the armchair he'd just vacated.

Then denial surged, pitching her forward. "This is preposterous. I know Petros loved me, but he loved you way more—God only knows why, or how he could love you at all. But how could he think that Dora would be better off with you rather than with me, who's been her other mother all along? How could he believe you'd make a better parent for her? I could have understood it if he wanted you to be her guardian, financially, though he also knew I'd need no help in that area."

She gulped down the agitation that threatened to suffocate her. "Though he never cared about money beyond being comfortable, maybe it was different when it came to his daughter. Maybe he wanted you to secure her future beyond anything I could afford. But to ask you to be her *father?* You of all people? Who never nurtured a living thing, not even a pet or a plant? You, who *hates* children?"

"I don't hate children. I never said I did. I said I would never have any. If it had been my choice, I wouldn't have. But this is no longer a matter of choice. Petros was specific in his will in what he needed me to be to Dorothea. And I will fulfill the terms of his will to the letter."

"And I say again, don't bother. I will have his will overturned. He was on death's door and not of sound mind when he had it written."

"He drew up his will seven months before the accident. As soon as Dorothea was born, in fact."

Naomi slumped back, the world collapsing around her like a burning building. "I don't believe you! If there is such a will at all, his attorney should have informed me of it, should have let me know of your alleged claim, since it directly clashes with mine."

"Petros used my attorney to draw up the will, and had it delivered directly to me. He told me not to inform you of it until it was possible for me to come do it in person."

Andreas approached her as he spoke, and she felt as if she was waiting for a tidal wave to crash on top of her and crush her.

Once in front of her, he bent smoothly. She lurched backward, unable to bear his physical closeness now, feeling she'd lose all control if he touched her.

He didn't. He just reached for the briefcase at her feet. Straightening, he opened it, produced a file. Bending once more, he placed it, opened, on her lap.

She tore her gaze from his, dragged it to what felt like a slab of ice on her legs, freezing every spark of warmth and life. Her vision blurred on the lines, as if to escape registering the evidence of his claims.

Then her focus sharpened, and every word she read struck her to her marrow with horror.

It was true. Every word he'd said. Apart from the framework of legalese, this was a letter from Petros, in his inimitable voice. Dated two days after Dora's birth. Signed unequivocally by him.

Suddenly, she felt she'd been stabbed through the heart. That Petros would bypass her in favor of Andreas, giving him Dora…Dora…*her baby.*

She closed the file with a trembling hand, shoved it to the table as if it burned her, and looked up at him, red-hot needles prickling at the back of her eyes.

Andreas was watching her intently, analyzing her reaction, documenting its every nuance. Didn't he already know how hard this blow would hit her?

He finally exhaled. "You're welcome to verify the will's authenticity."

"You mean if you wanted to fake a document, I'd have a prayer of proving it was a forgery?"

His head tilted, as if he was accepting praise. "I know for a fact no one would."

"Spoken like an expert counterfeiter. Forge anything major lately?"

"Not lately, no."

How blasé he was as he admitted to past and no doubt frequent fraud. But then, why not, when he was certain there was no possibility of exposure?

"But there's no forgery this time," he said. "This is authentic."

She gritted her teeth. "Why should I believe you?"

"What reason do I have for doing this, if it wasn't?"

"How should I know? No one in this world has any idea what goes on inside your mind, what drives you. For all I know you might be doing this to spite me."

"Contrary to what you seem to believe, I never wished to spite you. If anything, I only ever wished to do the opposite. I have clearly failed."

"Gee, I wonder why? Just *how* did Petros not only love and trust you, but will his daughter to you?"

"So you believe this is his will."

"I'd give anything for it not to be, but yes, I believe it." She dropped her head in her hands, feeling it would snap off her neck if she didn't. "The only reason I can think why Petros might have done this is that he thought it a precaution that would never come into play. He was your age, had every reason to think he'd live another fifty years."

"Actually, Petros discovered he had an inoperable heart condition two years after he married Nadine."

Naomi jerked her head up. "What?"

"Once he was diagnosed, he believed his father and grandfather had it, and it was why they died at around forty. Fearing the condition ran in his father's family, afflicting males only, when he and Nadine decided to resort to IVF through surrogacy, they ensured the gender of the baby to avoid the possibility of passing on the problem. He actually didn't want to have a child at all after he discovered his condition, hating to think he'd die and leave Nadine and his baby prematurely. But she wanted one so much, he had to do everything in his power to give her one. You know how impossible it was not to give Nadine what she wanted."

"But…but he never told her of his condition. If he did, she might have never persisted in having a baby."

"He did tell her. She just didn't tell *you*. She insisted that his condition might never threaten his life, and she wasn't letting it stop them from living their shared life to the fullest. She turned out to be right. It wasn't his condition that ended up killing him, but a drunk driver."

Naomi found herself on her feet again, mortification at being left in the dark tightening her every muscle until she felt they'd snap. "I can't believe she kept this from me!"

Andreas took a step closer. "Don't feel bad that the kid sister you believed shared everything with you kept something of this magnitude from you. I believe she made the right choice. By not telling you, she was refusing to acknowledge the whole thing, refusing to let it poison their daily lives. She felt she'd imposed on you enough to solve their conception problems, didn't want to burden you with a dread she'd decided to ignore. And she was right again. By pretending his condition didn't exist, she managed to give them that full life they craved together. While they lived."

Naomi stared at him, feeling as if she were plummeting into an alternate universe. She'd never heard Andreas talk so much. That was a week's worth of words in his book.

But it was the words themselves that bewildered her. And that there was an actual expression on his face, in his voice, as he'd said them. As if he was concerned, was trying to ameliorate her shock. Which was the most improbable thing in this whole situation.

"Is there more?" she finally whispered. "I'd

rather you hit me over the head with it all at once and get it done with, rather than prolong the ordeal."

His shrug said he had nothing more to relate. She didn't believe that. There was more, and he knew it all, but would tell her only what suited him.

But even in what he'd deemed to tell her, there were too many question marks. "So Petros believed he might not live long enough to be Dora's father, but there was no reason he'd fear for Nadine's life, too. How could he think of willing you to be Dora's father when her mother was around?"

"He wanted Dorothea to have more than just her mother. He wanted her to have a family."

"He didn't consider *me* family?"

"He thought it would be too much for you, being all the family Nadine and Dorothea had."

"I was *always* all the family Nadine had. And she was all my family, too, as Dora is now. How could he have thought I'd find it too much? What the hell did he think he was doing, deciding what I'm capable of, and making decisions for me?"

Andreas's gaze grew more serene, as if to counteract her rising agitation, and she wanted to hit him over the head with something. That file, preferably.

"Petros knew his wife, knew how dependent she was on you all your lives, the dependence she only partially transferred to him when they got married. He feared if he died, Nadine would be too destroyed to care for Dorothea properly. He believed she couldn't bring up a baby alone and would lean on you completely. He also knew you would have let her, would have supported her and Dorothea fully, at the expense of your own life. He didn't think it fair to you."

"Did he tell you all that?"

"Yes."

Naomi pressed trembling hands to her eyes as her voice quavered. "And he considered you the one qualified to carry Nadine's and Dora's burden? He thought you were equipped to deal with a bereaved woman and a fatherless baby? That you can become the first's pillar of strength and the second's stand-in father? Are you sure it was his heart that had something wrong with it and not his brain?"

"I didn't argue with him about my eligibility for the role he wanted me to play in the event of his death. I always did, and will always do, whatever he wanted, no questions asked."

"Are *you* out of your mind then, thinking you can

do what he asked you to do? You're not equipped to feel anything for anyone, let alone a baby, and a girl at that. And wait a minute! He wanted you to be her father, so she would have a family? How are you supposed to provide her with *that?*"

"As you pointed out earlier, I wasn't grown in a lab. I do have a family. A big one."

"A family you have nothing to do with, and have never been a part of. A family in name, but never in reality. A family you didn't even inform that you got married and divorced."

"For Petros's sake, for his daughter's, I'm willing to change that."

Feeling his calm, ready answers singeing her insides with oppression and frustration, she raised both hands, needing to abort this conversation and its possible catastrophic outcomes. "You don't have to go to the trouble of establishing a relationship with your family to give Dora one. Dora already has a family. Me, Hannah, Hannah's family, my friends and colleagues. She will grow up surrounded by people who love her, and she certainly doesn't need someone like you in her life, someone who knows nothing about emotions, nor cares anything about other people, let alone children."

As her last words rang in the room, he exhaled. "Are you done? I can stand here and listen to you enumerating my fatal flaws as long as you wish."

"How kind of you. Your every word is just another display of the depth of your insensitivity. But I'm done. And you're gone. Take that will with you and forget that Petros ever wrote it. Forget all about us."

"I can't. And I won't. Petros was my only friend, and his wishes are sacred to me. I will carry out his last will and testament, Naomi. There's nothing you can do to stop me."

"Don't be too sure about that. I don't care if that will is authentic. I will contest it. I will contest Petros's mental state at the time he made it. He thought he would die, and the validity of his decisions while under that conviction is questionable. And you can bet I will contest *you*. Any court would take one look at you and realize you're not father material. No judge would give you custody of Dora over me."

"Then you have no idea how family courts work. I am far richer and more powerful than you, than almost anyone. There's no contest. Any court would give me custody."

"We'll just have to see if they'll consider money

and status over the proof of existing emotional bonds and stability and previous healthy relationships."

"If it comes down to comparing pros and cons, I have what would tip the scale in my favor. Dorothea's father's direct endorsement. Do you have any such thing from your sister?"

That had Naomi's heart stopping for a terrible beat, before it detonated with a gush of dread. They'd never even *thought* of any provisions for a situation like this.

Even after Nadine was gone in the blink of an eye, Naomi had never thought her claim to Dora would ever be contested, let alone in jeopardy. And for the rival claim to be Andreas's! It was so preposterous she could almost believe this whole visit was a vivid nightmare.

But she would fight him to her last breath. Not because he would be snatching away the one thing she had to live for, but for Dora herself.

She told him so. "You might be able to trump my claim to Dora, but did you think what you'll do once she's yours? You, the ultimate example of emotional dysfunction? Dora would be better off in an orphanage than with you."

In answer, he bent, swept the file off the table,

and calmly put it back into the briefcase. "Again, Naomi, your opinion of me is irrelevant. As far as I am concerned, Dorothea is a Sarantos already. The rest is just formalities. Ones we can conclude with minimum conflict, for Dorothea's sake. Though she's very young, I'm sure she'd sense the discord if you turn this into a needless struggle."

Pivoting, he walked away now that it suited him, leaving destruction in his wake, as he always did.

Before he disappeared from the room that now felt like a battlefield, he drove icicles into her heart. "If you choose to do it the hard way, I'm ready for as long and as costly a battle as it would take. One you'll end up losing, anyway."

Four

"There's no doubt, Ms. Sinclair."

Naomi stared at the immaculate man, the regret on his face and in his voice making her heart give another painful thud against her ribs, before spiraling into her gut.

"Are you absolutely certain, Mr. Davidson?"

"Positive. Mr. Sarantos's claim is far stronger. He has a bona fide will from Dorothea's father, and you have nothing of equal strength in your favor. With his being who he is, no matter what you cite as your superior qualification as a parent or that you are her surrogate mother, his claim will have precedence. The one thing we could do is petition for you to remain a regular presence in the child's life, but that would also be at Mr. Sarantos's and the judge's discretion. Though I have no doubt we would get you generous visitation rights, as I don't see why Mr. Sarantos would contest them, since there's no dispute as there would be in a custody case after a divorce."

A scoff almost escaped Naomi. If only Mr. Davidson knew that with Andreas, anything was a dispute. He shredded his opponents on principle, even if he had nothing to gain by it. She had their divorce as solid proof of how vicious he could be, just because he could.

But her attorney had no idea, because he hadn't handled her divorce battle with Andreas. His daughter, Amara, had. Amara had been a good friend before becoming an attorney, and Naomi had trusted her to keep the divorce proceedings a total secret. As Andreas's own attorney had, since there hadn't been a word about their marriage or its dissolution in any media outlet. Not that she was about to enlighten Mr. Davidson now. At this point she felt any more information might be fuel that would burn any bridges to having Dora in her life at all.

She let out a shaky exhalation. "So in a fight, I don't stand a chance of keeping Dora?"

"As only her aunt, and with the will you describe, and with Mr. Sarantos's enormous influence, regretfully, no."

She'd already more than half known that, was here hoping against hope. Hearing the words still felt like a burning coal sliding down her throat.

Feeling she was pushing the lump of agony back out, she whispered, "Any advice?"

"Just this. Keep this out of court if you possibly can. Your best hope is not to antagonize Mr. Sarantos, but to appeal to him. His goodwill is all you can count on."

In an hour's time, she was staring in the mirror in her building's elevator.

Her reflection looked worse than what had looked back at her after she'd left Andreas four years ago. Or even after Nadine's death. Her complexion was mottled, the blue of her eyes was muddy, even the luster in her blond hair was gone. Two people who'd met her on the way from her attorney had been so alarmed they'd both thought she was ill. One had tried to convince her to let him take her to the emergency room.

The ping announcing her floor lurched through her, had her stumbling out of the elevator. At her apartment door, she stopped, her hand clenching the keys until it ached.

The delightful baby sounds coming from inside, which always lifted her heart even at its most leaden, only sank talons of misery in it now. It was unimaginable, unbearable, unsurvivable—the thought of losing Dora. A life without her constantly there, hers to love, to take care of and to worry about, wasn't worth living.

Leaning her clammy forehead on the cool wood, Naomi drew in a ragged breath, trying to suppress the tears that threatened to pour. She had to get her act together, couldn't walk in looking as if her world had ended. It had disturbed Dora when Naomi had been unable to control her anguish after Nadine's death, and she'd been only seven months old then. Now she was much more aware, and supremely sensitive to moods. Whenever a wave of desolation swept Naomi, it got to Dora bad. She couldn't expose her baby to her current condition.

God, this was all her fault. Everything had snowballed from the moment she'd allowed her desire for Andreas to overrule her logic and self-respect. And again, when she hadn't escaped with minimum damage that first time she'd walked away.

But when he'd eventually come after her and offered what she'd thought impossible with him, marriage, she'd fallen back into his arms.

Unable to break her addiction to him, she'd accepted his stunted proposal. She'd convinced herself it had been as close to a confession of involvement as she could expect from him, and consented to his abnormal terms. She hadn't even contested it when he'd stipulated their marriage would be a secret known only to them and Nadine and Petros, so his complicated business life wouldn't invade his private one. Their so-called wedding day had consisted of signing a few papers, then a meal with her sister and his friend, which Andreas hadn't even attended, having to leave before it started. Naomi hadn't let herself mind, especially when the wedding *night* had dragged her back into the depths of delirium.

Afterward, he'd remained insatiable, but true to his terms. He'd kept their marriage a secret he guarded to the point of obsession. Rationalizing his behavior had become the basis of her thinking, believing that it was natural for him to protect his private life at all costs. But that would have made sense if said life actually included her. And it hadn't.

Just like when they'd been only lovers, he hadn't let her enter his inner world. He'd never taken her to his home. She'd never even found out if he'd *had* a place he called home. They'd met in hotels or rentals, he'd never joined her in her personal places or endeavors, and they'd never even gone out together. He'd kept her strictly out of everything he'd done, personal or professional, told her nothing of his past and never mentioned the future.

The sum total of mentioning his family had been to admit that *the* Aristedes Sarantos was his brother. It had been how she'd found out—from *Aristedes's* scarce online info—that Andreas had a large family that included four sisters, with an assortment of nephews and nieces. He'd closed the subject of his family forever by claiming he had no relations with them whatsoever. While that seemed plausible, he might have said that just to end any possibility of her asking to meet them. Whatever the truth had been, she'd been certain of one thing. His family hadn't known she existed. She'd been right.

But while she and Andreas had continued leading separate lives, except during the constant sex sessions he'd seemed as addicted to as she'd been,

Nadine and Petros had become inseparable and had soon gotten married.

It had been the up-close example of their true intimacy and intense emotional bond that had broken the trance Naomi had placed herself in so she'd accept the conditions of her non-marriage to Andreas. Not that she'd given in easily. Whenever the need to share with Andreas something approaching what Nadine and Petros shared became unbearable, she'd reminded herself how different she and her sister were, how Andreas and Petros were opposites, and that their relationships were bound to be as dissimilar.

Then one day Nadine had told her of her and Petros's failed efforts to conceive, and that they'd seek professional help. Later that night, Naomi had mentioned that to Andreas. She would never forget his reaction. He'd turned to her, colder than she'd ever seen him and said that if she thought relating that to imply it was time *they* had a baby, she could forget it. He was *never* having children.

His icy declaration had finally forced her to face the pathetic emptiness of their relationship. He'd underscored the fact that if she remained with him, she'd have nothing to look forward to but more of the same nothingness. And it *had* been her fault yet again. She should have known she wouldn't be able to withstand that unnatural arrangement with the emotionally aberrant man that he was for long, let alone forever. Not only hadn't there been any hope for anything more between them, they'd never had *anything* to start with. She'd never felt like his wife, and he'd certainly been no husband to her. Apart from being his "sexual habit," she hadn't existed to him.

Next day she'd asked him for a divorce. Thinking he'd be as nonreactive as he'd been the first time she'd tried to end their liaison, she'd been shocked by his fury. He'd seethed, saying that he wouldn't be coerced into giving her what she wanted. Her anger had risen to match his. What had he thought she wanted? A real marriage, God forbid? He'd retorted that she'd known exactly what to expect, and she'd agreed. She wouldn't make him the villain.

Heart breaking, she'd asked for one thing, the first and last thing she'd ever ask from him. A quick and hassle-free divorce, to end what they should never have started.

When he'd again watched her leave in silence, she'd been certain he wouldn't come after her this time. And he hadn't. He'd just sent his legal hound to snap at her feet and drag her through six months of struggle and anxiety before he'd deigned to let her go.

If it weren't for her pursuing Andreas in the first place, then going back for more when she should have run, Nadine wouldn't have met Petros. None of the chain reaction of catastrophes ending in the current one would have occurred.

But then, Dora wouldn't have come into existence, either. And for her alone, Naomi would never wish anything different.

Now she had to figure out how to keep her from Andreas's cold grasp.

Straightening, she filled her lungs with air. The plunge into the past, as mortifying and self-condemning as it had been, had had a good side effect. It had driven away her desperation, dried her eyes and steadied her nerves.

After another bracing breath, she walked into her apartment.

Entering the family room where Andreas's echoes still lingered, she found Dora sitting on the floor by her playpen, playing catch-whatever-I-throw-to-you with Hannah. Loki and Thor, their mink and flame point Ragdoll cats, were curled up on the couch, watching them.

Though Naomi's feet made no sound on the plush

carpeting she'd installed throughout the apartment in time for Dora's very active crawling phase, the baby turned around as soon as she walked in. And Naomi's lungs emptied once again.

Meeting Dora's sky-blue eyes across the distance, imagining again she was looking into Nadine's, would have been enough to knock the breath out of her. But the instant delight, the total trust and dependence she saw in them overwhelmed her barely restored control. Tears stung her eyes as Dora let out a squeal, threw down her toys and scooted on all fours toward her. The cats followed at a slower strut.

"Darling, oh my darling…"

The all-encompassing love she felt for Dora, the baby she'd carried for nine months in her womb, whose heartbeats and kicks she'd felt inside her own body, who'd been the focus of her life since her first wail, and who was all that remained of her beloved Nadine, came pouring out. She rushed to snatch her up, fiercely hugging her precious body.

Dora squealed as her plump arms grasped her neck, her face mashing into her shoulder.

Naomi buried her own face in the raven silk of Dora's hair, inhaling the sweetness of her baby scent, her heart trembling with the totality of emotions she felt for her.

After giving them time to enjoy their tête-a-tête, Hannah rose from the floor, her smile wide…until she met Naomi's eyes.

Her smile faltering, Hannah injected her voice with brightness for Dora's sensitive ears, even when her words were anxious. "What's wrong, Naomi? Did something happen at work?" Then she seemed to make the connection. "Is it something to do with Mr. Sarantos's visit yesterday?"

Naomi debated telling her the truth, and decided against it. No point upsetting Hannah, too, when there was nothing she could do about it but fret sooner than she had to.

Trying to clear the anguish from her expression, she attempted a smile. "It's just that seeing him seemed to rewind everything…the accident, their deaths. Made me feel it all just happened."

Hannah sighed, caressing Naomi's back soothingly. "It will keep creeping up on you, for years. Sometimes it will come out of the blue, but mostly it will be seeing people or things or places that you associate with Nadine or Petros that will trigger it. But from my experience with losing loved ones, especially after my Ralph's death, I can as-

sure you it will get better with time. And one day
the good memories will become stronger, will be
what come to you when you think of Nadine, making you happy to remember."

Naomi's smile almost shattered as she nodded,
fondling and cooing to Dora. Dora cooperated for
a minute more before she started wriggling, demanding to be put down. With one last kiss and
nuzzle of her downy cheek, Naomi obliged.

Once on the ground, Dora zoomed away with
the utmost zeal and determination, the cats in tow.
She stopped after a few feet, sat back to check that
Naomi was following, too, her chubby hand opening and closing, demanding she hurry.

A laugh bubbled out of Naomi at the baby's earnest expression. Dora took playing very seriously
indeed.

She rushed to obey her imperative demand, and
for the next two hours, she reveled in all the things
that were now the center of her universe, its emotional glue—the play, feeding and bath time with
Dora.

After putting her down to sleep at eight, Naomi
declined Hannah's offer of watching a movie on
the grounds that she had work to finish, and entered her study. She sat at her desk, staring into

nothingness for what felt like an hour, her attorney's words echoing in her head.

Your best hope is not to antagonize Mr. Sarantos, but to appeal to him. His goodwill is all you can count on.

It was way too late for that advice. She'd already antagonized Andreas and then some. And appeal to his goodwill? If this was all she could count on, then she was doomed.

An unstoppable impulse had her reaching for her cell phone, keying in his number. It might not be working after all these years, but it was the only one she'd ever had for him.

"Naomi."

His deep, electrifying voice poured right into her brain after a single ring.

How did he know it was her? Her number was new, and only the people closest to her knew it.

But why was she even wondering? There was probably nothing about her that he didn't know.

God. Why had she called him? She should hang up, bundle up Dora and Hannah and board the first flight to anywhere. Disappear until he got bored again, and just let them be.

Yeah, right. As if he ever let anything go without first sucking it dry of whatever he wanted.

Only then would he let go. He'd move on, like a hurricane always did, only after it had destroyed everything.

"You can call back when you're ready to talk."

His patient suggestion zapped through her, sparking her ire. "Sorry if I'm interrupting something important."

As soon as she said that, the malignant images assailed her again, as they had since she'd left him. Images of Andreas with other women…

"I am actually between important things."

Which could mean he was between a brunette and a redhead.

After all, he'd once admitted that, before her, he'd never been attracted to blondes.

Not that she thought he was in a babe sandwich right now. He would have told her if he were. He was just being himself, the man who'd never offer gallantries, such as claiming that nothing was more important than her.

But knowing he'd always hit her with the truth in its most unadorned form was what made her despair. He said nothing he didn't mean. If he said he'd take Dora away, he would.

"I was heading for the shower," he explained.

"Then by all means." She barely stopped from suggesting he instead fill the tub…and drown in it.

Another patient sound poured into her ear, something that resembled a sigh. "I can stay on the line until you decide to tell me why you called."

The forbearance in his voice snapped the last thread of control. "I called to tell you that you are a monster, Andreas. And don't tell me it's my prerogative to see you as I please. This is not a point of view, this is a fact."

She could almost see him incline his head in assent. "As you wish. Anything else?"

So much crowded inside her, protests, pleas, scalding invective. Out loud she found herself saying, "So where are you holed up on your victorious return to New York?"

"You know where I am."

Suddenly, she was certain she did know. The Plaza.

Their first night had been all over the royal suite there. The memories of that transfiguring night had been why she'd once intimated she preferred its ambience to all hotels. They'd met there whenever he was in downtown New York from then on, even when she'd insisted the place was too expensive, too *much* for only them. He'd disregarded her protests. Later, she'd found he owned a big chunk of the hotel and paid nothing. She would have appreciated the explanation, so she wouldn't have felt so wasteful. As always, she hadn't warranted one.

Not that he could be there for sentimental reasons. It was most probably for the anonymity the establishment had always been eager to provide him.

"Still there as Thomas Adler or Jared Mathis or one of the other aliases you parade under?" she asked.

When she'd discovered his pseudonymous activities, he'd briefly explained that while people unavoidably recognized him in public, he made sure no one could trace his whereabouts. Such meticulous evasions had never made sense to her. She would have understood his obsessive security measures, if he didn't walk around *without* any.

"I'm here as myself."

The unexpected response skewered through her heart.

If security had ever been the motive, he was an even bigger target now, being so much richer and more successful and having far more enemies. That left her old suspicions as the only explanation. All that secrecy *had* been on her account. So no one would associate him with her. He'd never wanted a wife or even a steady lover, and he'd gone the extra thousand miles so it wouldn't be known he'd had either, keeping his image as an icy womanizer untarnished.

Without one more word, she ended the call.

There was nothing more to be said, anyway.

It was time for action.

Fifteen minutes later, she was staring at the achingly familiar door of the Plaza's royal suite.

It felt as if she'd been here only yesterday for yet another rendezvous with Andreas. The concierge had rushed to receive her, the same man from her visits four years ago. The one Andreas had entrusted with keeping his stays and their meetings a secret. With a gushing welcome that seemed genuine, he'd given her a key card to access the exclusive floor and suite. It seemed Andreas had never bothered to rescind his orders to extend to her the same privileges he commanded.

Putting the key card away, she rang the bell.

In a minute, the door opened. And all her systems almost suffered an instantaneous shutdown.

Andreas stood there, hair gleaming, white shirt wide-open and faded jeans hanging dangerously low on his hips. Everything she'd seen encased in his suit yesterday, then felt against her body, was on display. He seemed even taller barefoot, his shoulders so wide they blocked out her world. His torso and abdomen were a sleek, mouthwatering sculpture of muscle sheathed in polished skin dusted with the perfect amount of bronze silk. Everything else was a composite of pure power and masculinity molded to perfection.

His steel eyes penetrated her as he stood aside, his motion like a magnet pulling her across the threshold. He stalked barely a foot behind as she walked into the oval foyer that led to an array of social and private rooms. Soon she was walking into the living room, barely noticing its rich decorations, sumptuous textiles and exquisite furnishings that she vaguely remembered were inspired by the royal court of Louis XV. All she knew was that every inch of this place echoed with memories, of when he'd taken her and pleasured her, in its every nook, in every way.

Just inside the huge room, she turned around to face him, found him watching her with that intensity that had always melted her. It now made her feel besieged, fenced in, even in the almost five thousand square foot suite.

"I calculated you'd let a day pass before you came," he said, his voice thrumming every inflamed nerve. "When you called, I adjusted that to an hour. You're earlier than all my estimates. It's a good thing I decided not to shower before—"

She slapped him. So hard her palm went numb with pain.

Horrified at her action, she watched the imprint of her hand form then evaporate on his chiseled cheek.

His only response was a calm "Don't hit me again, Naomi."

"Or what?"

His eyes told her exactly what.

Feeling as if it wasn't her doing this, in slow motion, announcing her intention with absolute clarity, she raised her other hand and slapped his right cheek.

His eyes remained open, roasting her alive. "I'll step out of your reach now, Naomi. Just in case you don't know what you're inviting."

Her hands bunched in his open shirt, all her agony and dread and yearning boiling over. His gaze devoured her, but his body remained inert, refusing to respond to her fury, leaving it up to her to slam into him.

She did, and it was as if she'd hit a wall, one that buzzed with a million volts of magnetism and maleness. She yanked on his shirt, trying to get him to respond. He just looked down at her, doing everything to her with his eyes, but letting her know he wouldn't give her what she was after...yet.

Taking her incursion further, she groped for his hair, sank her fingers in its silky depths and tugged. A hiss escaped his thinned lips, a testament to her roughness and his enjoyment of it. Surging on tiptoes, she dragged his head down, her lips gasping for his, parched, unable to withstand those last seconds before he quenched years' worth of thirst.

But it seemed he still needed more. He would not accept any demonstration that would have him meet her halfway. Her offer wasn't total enough yet for his liking, what would later make her fully accountable for her actions and decisions. By holding back, he was letting her know he would share none of the responsibility for them...as usual. His role was to tempt and inflame. It was up to her to throw herself into his inferno. Like that first time...and from then on.

Mind gone, body ablaze, she was ready to go to any lengths, whatever the consequences, just so he'd take her over, expose her to the full power of his passion. Not knowing what would satisfy him, she rubbed breasts aching for his possession against his chest, undulated the core weeping for his invasion against his hardness.

Suddenly, it felt as if his whole body expanded when he dragged her head back by her hair, and his breath, fresh and potent, filled her tight lungs as his snarl scorched her lips.

"That's it, Naomi, that's *exactly* it."

Then he smashed his lips down on hers.

It was like a dam had burst, flooding her with what she'd never experienced except with him. Oneness. Need that sliced her open, left her begging for everything...*everything.*

Her senses went off like fireworks with the delight of reconnection as he gave her the ravaging she'd been starving for. Her whimpers became incessant as his teeth sank into her lips, as his tongue drove inside her mouth, occupying her, draining her.

Then he snatched his lips away. The letdown buckled her legs, but he was only taking his onslaught to the next level. Pressing her to the wall, his hands roamed all over her, tearing every stitch of clothes from her burning body, his every move loaded with the precise ruthlessness of a starving predator unleashed on a prey long kept out of reach.

His pupils flared, turning his eyes black as her breasts spilled into his palms. His homage to them was brief but devastating before he was on his knees, dragging her panties off, burying his lips in her core, diving into her flowing readiness. She hovered on the edge of orgasm; one more sweep of his hot tongue or graze of his teeth would finish her. But she didn't want release. She wanted *him*.

"Please…"

He understood her need, as he always had. He heaved up, caught her plea in his savage mouth. He ravaged her lips as he lifted her, his large hands locking her feet around his buttocks, sending her heartbeat stampeding at his effortless strength. Then he freed his erection.

Another plea choked out of her depths as his length teased her swollen flesh, sending a million arrows of pleasure to her womb. He glided his incredible heat and hardness through the molten lips of her core, from her bud to her opening, just once. On the next sweep, he rammed inside her, sinking in her to the hilt.

The savagery and abruptness of his invasion was

a shock so acute, her heart faltered and she collapsed in his hold.

He growled something ferocious, what she thought was "Too long...too damn long..." His teeth sank into her shoulder, like a lion tethering his mate for a jarring ride. Then he withdrew.

It felt as if he was dragging her life force out with him, and her arms tightened around his neck, her hands clawing at him, begging for his return. He complied, responding with an even harder, deeper plunge, blacking out all her senses with the searing fullness, the beyond-her-limits expansion around his girth and length. Then he set her on fire as his thrusts picked up the tempo.

Every withdrawal was maddening loss, every plunge excruciating ecstasy. Her cries blurred into wails, her flesh yielding fully to his invasion. He muttered her name in a litany, each thrust accentuated by the carnal sounds of their flesh slapping together. The scents of sex and abandon were like an aphrodisiac, the glide and burn of his hard flesh inside her stoking the inferno of pleasure until she felt she'd combust. She needed...needed... Please...please...*please*...

As always, realizing what she needed, when and how hard and fast she needed it, he hammered his hips between her splayed thighs, his erection pounding inside her with the cadence and force to unleash the conflagration that would consume her, until one thrust breached her womb and shattered the coil of need.

Her body detonated, from where he was buried deepest outward, merciless currents of release crashing through her, squeezing her around him, choking her shrieks.

Roaring her name, he fed her convulsions with his own climax, jetting the burning fuel of his pleasure on hers, filling her to overflowing, sharpening the throes of release, until she slumped in his arms, sated, replete, complete.

Before consciousness fully returned, she heard him groan, "Not enough, *agápi mou...*"

Boneless in his hold, like a marionette with all her strings cut, her head spun as his endearment echoed inside her. My love...or my darling. What he only ever said during sex.

Then the world was thudding with the urgency of his strides. She drifted off for what might have been seconds or an hour, jerking out of the sensual stupor as she felt him laying her down on the bed where he'd once owned her. His scent rose from the silk sheets to wrap around her, compensating her for his loss as he left her body.

He retreated only to rid himself of his clothes, before coming back over her, impacting her with his demand.

Spreading her quivering thighs, bending her knees, he braced his at the bed's edge and bore down on her, pinning her by the shoulders. Then, bending to thrust his tongue inside her panting mouth, he reentered her in a long, burning plunge.

She'd thought he'd drained her of every need, that she'd want nothing ever again. But as he forged inside her, and her sore, swollen tissues expanded around his daunting girth, urgency slammed into her once more, her awakened flesh clamoring harder, louder.

After that first frenzied coupling, he took her in a deliberate yet even more gloriously raw possession. Throughout, he exploited every inch of her body with hands and lips and teeth. And he watched her. Oh, the way he watched her.

His feral focus made it all more primal and mind-blowing, making every touch a bolt of ecstasy, every bite and dig and thrust a howling pleasure.

Soon, unable to stand any more stimulation, she climaxed again, four years of deprivation exploding into torrents of sensation, even fiercer than the first firestorm. At her peak, he rode her harder, faster, till he rammed himself into her recesses, roaring as he hurled himself after her into the abyss of abandon. Her whole body shook with ecstasy as his hardness pulsed inside her, shooting his essence, her over-sensitized muscles fluttering around him, greedily milking him for every drop of satisfaction.

This time, as her consciousness flickered, he sank on top of her, his breathing as labored as hers, his heart thundering against her sputtering one, completing her domination.

At last, he rose off her, swept her enervated form up to the pillows and contained her in the cloak of his great body.

After long minutes of lying there, savoring the descent, painting her savagely pleasured body with indolent caresses, he pulled himself up on one elbow and looked down at her, his gaze one of supreme male triumph and possession.

"Now that I've gulped you down twice, it's time to savor you."

She blinked dazedly up at him, shocked to find her body readying itself for him again. This sickness had never been cured. If anything, it had intensified.

He reached over her to his cell on the bedside table, suckled one marvelously sore nipple soothingly as he offered the phone to her. "Tell Mrs. McCarthy you won't be home tonight."

Naomi's throat tightened. "I have to go home."

"No, you don't. And won't. I'm just getting started."

She pushed against him feebly, drowning as he resumed suckling and fondling her. "Andreas, stop. We have to talk."

"Talking is definitely not on my to-do list tonight. I might consider it tomorrow. Or the day after."

"Andreas...please, we must talk first."

He lifted his head from her breast, smile indulgent. "About this?"

"About Dora."

The heat in his eyes drained away. In two seconds, they were as cold as she'd ever seen them. Then without one more word or look, he released her and rose from the bed.

Every muscle feeling like jelly, she scrambled for the bedcovers as she watched him pull on his jeans.

Then he turned his unfathomable eyes to her.

"Was that what this was all about? Dorothea? What did you think you were achieving here? Bribing me?"

"I gave you what you came blackmailing me for."

"I don't remember any blackmail."

"It was implied, loud and clear."

"Then you forgot all about me. Or never knew much about me at all. I never imply anything. If I wanted to blackmail you, I would have spelled out my ultimatum 'loud and clear.'"

Feeling hope for a way out quickly fading, she gasped, "It was, to me. You made your sexual interest patent, then told me you'd take Dora. When you *know* I'd do anything to keep her."

"Even throw yourself in the shark's bed, eh? So what was your scenario? That I was here to extort you for vengeance sex, and once you gave me a mind-blowing send-off, I'd walk away and forget all about Petros's will, which I never considered seriously, anyway, but was only holding to your head?"

"What else could I think? You *can't* be considering taking on Dora for real," Naomi cried, feeling her world being ripped from under her as his stony glance told her he considered nothing else. "For God's sake, Andreas, you *know* you don't want a baby, and won't be able to give her the home and family life she needs and deserves."

He shrugged. "Probably. Even definitely. That's why I don't intend to take Dorothea from you."

Her heart surged with hope. "Y-you don't?"

He moved then, coming back to where she sat stiff and tangled in his covers. Leaning down on one knee, he made the mattress dip, tumbling her toward him, and murmured, "I don't."

Before she collapsed back with relief, his hand slipped beneath the sheets and cupped her breast, giving it a delicious squeeze. "I do intend to take you, though."

Her breast swelling in his large, warm palm, she moaned, "Don't you have it in reverse? I already slept with you."

He removed the sheet, engulfed the nipple that had been envying its twin in his hot mouth and pulled hard, making her moan and arch up. "You thought a couple of rolls in the royal suite would be all it took?"

Resigned that she'd end up giving in to his conditions, and temptation, she asked, "How many 'rolls' would it take?"

He raised his head and one eyebrow. "I can name any number?" At her grudging nod, his lips twisted. "How many would do it, do you think? Considering my record of insatiability with you? I must have had you over a thousand times during our time together, and it failed to sate me."

"It sure won't be anywhere near as many as that!"

"You won't consider an unlimited usage arrangement? Pity."

"Oh, fine. Whatever you want."

At her sullen capitulation, he withdrew, rose from the bed and stood over her, studying her molten pose.

Then, thumbs hooked into his jeans, eyes enigmatic, he exhaled. "The thing is, Naomi, what I want is something a bit more significant than even your limitless sexual services."

She struggled up, numb with dread, cold with outrage and flaming with desire all at once. "What could that be? My soul?"

He waved his hand. "You can keep your soul. I only want everything else. What you'll give me when you remarry me."

Five

Where the hell was her other shoe?

Naomi limped around, frantically looking for the damned thing. Where *had* that *damned* man tossed it?

She might be looking right at it and not seeing it. And that wouldn't be strange. Everything had been a blur since Andreas had made his outrageous proposition.

Following an interminable period of gaping at him, she'd exploded from the bed and run out to retrieve her clothes. She was one shoe away from fleeing this place, and hurtling in search of any way to keep that tormentor at bay.

Remarry him, indeed!

Her sanity and self-respect had barely survived marrying him the first time.

What shocked her most was that he'd never wanted to marry her at all. He'd wed her only as a means to keep an "accommodating" sexual partner placated so she wouldn't leave. He didn't view marriage as other human beings did. So why would he—

"It's beneath the divan. The three-seater."

Whirling around at the sound of his calm voice, she found him still in only his jeans, leaning one formidable shoulder against the archway into the expansive room.

A stifled imprecation escaped her as she lunged for the shoe she only saw when he'd told her where to look. She *had* looked there before and hadn't seen it.

In seconds she had it on, then snatched her purse off the same divan, where he'd thrown it what felt like a lifetime ago. Cursing under her breath again, she headed toward the escape route he was blocking.

He let her come within a foot before he uncoiled and filled the archway. It would be impossible to pass him without physical contact. She knew full well where that would lead.

She raised her eyes to his. "Move aside, please, and let's not turn this into a worse mess than it already is."

"I take it all this flouncing about is your way of saying 'hell, no'?"

"Flouncing!" She reined back her indignation. This man was turning out to be an expert provocateur, a quality he'd never demonstrated before, but seemed to be taking much pleasure in now. Since it was so unexpected, she'd been an easy mark, letting his every yank pull her wherever he wanted. But this stopped now.

Exhaling, she tried to access her control, as fractured as it was, and attempt to do what she hadn't done so far—take her emotions out of the equation and talk pure sense.

"Listen, Andreas, we do share an unhealthy level of sexual affinity, as we just proved…." Her gaze flicked to the wall a few feet away, where he'd taken her the first time tonight. "And that was why 'our past' happened. I take full responsibility for how it turned out, as I was young, more in experience than in actual age, and you were my first adventure, my first passion. You were as clear as possible about what you expected, and I still mixed up my intense lust for you with expectations that had no place between us."

His focus was total as she talked, as if he was memorizing her words. But then he did that with everything. His retentive powers were phenomenal, and it had nothing to do with interest in her or what she said specifically.

She inhaled. "But since you made *your* expectations clear from the start, you didn't accept it when I walked out. You no doubt thought you were justified in trying to stop me, as I was reneging on the terms of our agreement. I'm the first to admit I did, and that was why I ended it. Now you have a card to pressure me into rectifying my transgression and resuming the arrangement you found so convenient, but I can't 'accommodate' you anymore. I *am* ready, though, to have as much no-strings sex with you as you want, in return for you not disrupting Dora's life. We both have the obvious to gain from that kind of arrangement. Anything else is out of the question."

"Why?"

That was all he had to say? After all she'd said?

Holding on to her temper, she forced herself to answer. "Because I won't enter another charade with you. Certainly never with Dora caught in the middle."

"There was no charade tonight. That was all too real."

"As real as these things get. You know it was just sex."

"There's nothing 'just' about it. That after all these years I still want you."

"And you can have me. Just not like *that*."

"Again I ask, why? If you want me as much as I want you?"

"Because desire never made a difference. I wanted you at times more than I wanted to breathe, and yet being with you was the worst chapter of my life. Considering that I lived through the horror and desolation of losing my mother when I was so young, then losing Nadine, that gives you an idea of just how miserable I was with you."

That emptiness in his eyes intensified. And suddenly she realized something.

That blankness was a unique indicator of his emotions. The more surprised or dismayed he was, the emptier his gaze became.

Which made no difference now. Or ever. Only one thing mattered. Making him take back his demand.

Struggling to keep her voice level, she continued. "Agreeing to something as disruptive to me as what you're demanding would damage me and undermine my ability to mother Dora. And that's what I will never let happen."

After looking at her as if he wouldn't answer, he let out a forcible exhalation. "If you're willing to sleep with me as frequently and for as long as I want, why is calling it marriage any more disruptive?"

"Because it would be. Labels and legalities and the life adjustments stemming from them complicate everything. No-strings sex is all I can offer you. It's all you want, anyway."

"I already told you what I want. Marriage."

Now it was her turn to ask. "Why?"

He shrugged. "Because I'm not in the market for no-strings sex anymore. I have Dorothea now."

"No, you *don't*. Dora isn't yours, she's mine."

"Not according to Petros's will."

Anxiety and aggression almost overpowered her. She reeled them back with all she had.

Andreas *was* a shark, and the scent of blood—her vulnerability and desperation now—would only make him more vicious.

But appealing to his compassion, as her attorney had advised, would get her nowhere, either, as he had none.

Only one thing remained. Appealing to his paramount sense of self-service, what had seen him to the top in his cutthroat field.

She drew in a steadying breath. "It's clear you haven't thought this through, Andreas. You might assume that having a child, with your power and wealth, would be easy. But there's nothing more disruptive and consuming than having a little one in your life, even with others handling the daily caretaking. If you consider it without the influence of duty or pride..." She swallowed the words *"or challenge."* Not prudent to provoke his cold-blooded killer instinct. "...you'd know you can't take on the responsibility of a child."

"I know I can't. I already admitted that."

"Then what do you think you'd do if you take Dora? Toss her to a nanny and a string of private tutors, then send her off to an exclusive boarding school once she's old enough, and go about your business as if she doesn't exist?"

"I already told you this isn't what I intend. I never factored in that I won't have you both."

She gaped at him. He'd intended this remarriage thing all along? A "convenience package" that would allow him to have her cake and eat Dora's, too?

She swallowed the outrage, emptied her voice of expression. "Well, start factoring it in now. You have my offer."

He inclined his head, as if he accepted her refusal.

Then he stepped aside to let her pass.

Feeling as if her prison door had opened, she hurried away. He followed at a slower pace, his longer strides keeping him a step away, making her struggle not to break into a run.

She was almost out the door when he said, "I'll have my chauffeur follow you home."

She shook her head without turning. "The area is safe, and it's only a five-minute drive."

"Still."

Something in his solitary word made her turn. And she regretted it at once. Getting another eyeful of his half-naked grandeur, and remembering what he'd done to her with it, wasn't conducive to her ability to breathe.

He took the door from her hand. "I would have done it myself, but we've had enough arguments tonight."

Suddenly she was clasped to his hot hardness,

and his lips were pulling her heartbeats right out of her pulse point. Her blood surged with need, and she was on the verge of begging him to take her again when he muttered into her flesh.

Once his words sank in, she tore out of his arms. "You *are* a monster."

This time she ran away, as if she were really escaping from one.

After a night that was one of her life's worst, Naomi arrived at her office next morning, the last words Andreas had said still echoing in her head in a maddening loop.

Whatever you felt about our marriage, or think you feel about me now, you'll end up agreeing to my terms. I'm not letting you go again.

The first thing she did was call her attorney. He assured her again that she had no leverage, that Andreas would be the one to call the shots. She bet if she told him about Andreas's ultimatum, he would have thought it a fantastic offer she should snap up before Andreas changed his mind.

Not that she thought he would. Once Andreas set his mind to something, he never let go. But she was damned if she'd let him steamroll over her. There *had* to be another way out.

After an hour of frantic thinking, an idea burst into her mind. The more she thought about it, the more it felt like her only hope. Gaining an ally who was as powerful as Andreas, one who had power over him.

Only one man on earth met both criteria.

Andreas's older brother, Aristedes Sarantos.

An hour later, Naomi entered Sarantos Shipping headquarters, suffering from whiplash at the speed with which this meeting had been arranged.

After failing to find a personal number for Aristedes, she'd settled for his headquarters, gone through the automated menu until finally a live person, a man named Dennis, had regretted there was no way she'd get hold of Aristedes himself. Some collected voice in her churning mind had inspired her to say it was a matter of paramount urgency, concerning Aristedes's brother. At the silence her claim had been met with, she'd thought the man had hung up. Then Dennis had said that Mr. Sarantos's brother was long dead.

That had stunned her, that Aristedes might not know that his brother was alive.

But Dennis had rushed to apologize. She must have meant Mr. *Andreas*, not Mr. Leonidas. He hadn't heard of him in so long, he didn't remember him right away.

That had been news to Naomi, that Andreas had a brother named Leonidas, who was dead. He'd never volunteered the fact, and she'd never heard it from Petros, the only other source of information on him. Petros had clearly been under strict instructions not to share anything about Andreas, even with his wife. The only way she'd known anything about his family life had been through investigating Aristedes. But beyond a fleeting internet search once, she hadn't been about to dig any deeper into what Andreas hadn't wanted her to know.

Once Andreas's name had been introduced, she'd been put through to Aristedes's personal assistant. Within minutes, the woman had come back to her. Aristedes could meet her in half an hour. Would that be soon enough for her?

She'd almost blurted out it was too soon. Thinking that securing an audience with Aristedes would be an arduous endeavor, she'd thought she'd have time to prepare for meeting the man. If Andreas was anything to go by, she cringed to think what his big brother might be like, the man everyone mentioned in whispers of awe and called "the raw material of ruthlessness."

But she couldn't postpone meeting the only man in existence who might be able to hold Andreas at bay.

And here she was, in his imposing skyscraper's lobby, not knowing where to go or what to do.

As she swept her uncertain gaze around, a gorgeous dark-eyed brunette in her early twenties, a little shorter than her five foot seven, in an exquisite navy blue skirt suit, came rushing toward her.

"Ms. Sinclair?" Naomi nodded dumbly in answer to the woman's inquiring smile, noticing that she was older than she'd first surmised. Maybe thirty, like her, but untouched by tragedy. The woman's smile widened, showing off a stunning set of teeth as she held out her hand. "I'm Cora Delaney, Mr. Sarantos's junior PA. Please come with me. He is waiting for you."

Cora steered Naomi through security, then to a private elevator, seeming in a hurry.

Oh, God, was she late? What if this started the whole thing off on the wrong foot? How *could* she start this on the right one? What was she doing here, anyway? What *would* she tell Aristedes?

"Relax."

Her gaze jerked to Cora, and only then realized she was clutching the railing in the elevator car, her white knuckles stark against the mahogany walls.

Sympathy filled the secretary's eyes. "Mr. Sarantos can be really scary when he wants to, I'll admit, but he rarely wants to nowadays. Today is certainly not one of the days anyone is in danger of being shredded by him."

"What makes today special?" Naomi croaked.

Cora's smile widened. "He's expecting Mrs. Sarantos, his wife."

Mrs. Sarantos. Naomi had once been that. Not that anyone had ever known. Now she was here in hope of never becoming that again, whether people knew about it this time or not.

The elevator door whirred open smoothly. They were there. In the lion's den. Or was it the devil's domain? She'd once heard it would be bad-mouthing the devil, calling Aristedes Sarantos that.

A minute later, Cora ushered her to what had to be Aristedes's inner sanctum, clearly not intending to accompany her, and Naomi's knees almost gave out. She was used to interacting with moguls, but this man, from what she'd heard about him and especially because of who he was to Andreas, unnerved her as nothing had before. And she hadn't even seen him yet.

Then she did.

Rounding the corner of the waiting room, she spotted him at the far end of the austerely elegant office, rising from a spaceship-like desk. Even across the distance, his impact almost made her feet gnarl.

She'd seen him in photos, had thought him photogenic, but in reality, he was far, far more incredible. Like Andreas, nothing but in-person exposure could do him justice. He wasn't handsome. It would be an insult to call him, or Andreas for that matter, that. They were beautiful in a way that transcended good looks, were the embodiment of unadulterated power and raw maleness in human form.

Beyond that, they had the same color of eyes and skin, but Aristedes's hair was darker, with silver-shot temples, whereas the highlights in Andreas's hair were the gilded touch of the sun.

There was no doubt those two juggernauts were brothers. Even with eight years between them, the differences were slight, physically speaking. On another level, there was a major difference that she sensed, but couldn't put her finger on. And probably wouldn't.

As Aristedes unfurled to his full height, which appeared equal to Andreas's, her observations stalled. He was unsmiling as he walked around his desk, his steel eyes as penetrating and unsettling as Andreas's, even if their disturbance had a different texture. She could feel him reaching inside her to extract the truth about her and about her claim that she had urgent business concerning his estranged brother.

Before he came within hand-shaking distance, she heard a soft knock. It was followed by a gently opening door, rustling clothes and light feet on the plush carpet.

It had to be his wife.

Feeling like an intruder, Naomi kept her eyes fixed on Aristedes. And got a direct hit of the spectacular change that came over his face.

It was as if his deepest recesses opened, every passion and emotion blazing in his eyes. His delight at the sight of his wife was blinding.

"Selene, *agápi mou*..."

Agápi mou. One of the empty endearments Andreas had lavished on her...only at the height of arousal or the pinnacle of satisfaction. But from the ragged edge in Aristedes's bass voice, she had no doubt *he* meant it. His wife, the lucky Selene, *was* his love.

With a brief excuse, he strode past Naomi.

She didn't want to witness the greeting of this man who'd probably left his wife's side this morning, and yet was already so elated and eager to see her. But standing there with her back to the woman might be construed as rude. So she forced herself to turn around…and caught the tail end of the passionate kiss the couple exchanged.

Aristedes's lips relinquished his wife's, only to return immediately for another brief but profound taste. Then, after one last look full of all the secrets and trials and certainties that constituted their intimacy, he turned his attention to Naomi.

And she realized what the major difference between him and Andreas was. Even though she felt the demons of his harsh beginnings on the quays of Crete lurking within his psyche, to be unleashed when needed, she felt Aristedes had mastered them and relegated them to the deepest corner of his being. This man had reclaimed himself from the darkness. He was something Andreas had never been and would never be. He was serene, content. Happy.

And it was clear this hadn't happened only *for* Selene, but with her help, and was maintained by her unstinting support. A man of Aristedes's caliber didn't develop that level of emotional involvement and dependence without total trust in an equal, who offered him a commitment of matching depth, scope and strength. From the fleeting yet unequivocal demonstration she'd witnessed, Naomi had no doubt Aristedes would lay down his life for his wife, and that his devotion was reciprocated in full.

Her instincts had once told her she could share that level of allegiance with Andreas. Even against all evidence to the contrary, her senses had insisted they'd turn out to be right. But he'd proved to be exactly what he himself had warned her he was—a man incapable of emotional commitment and unworthy of it.

So how could two brothers who were so alike in genetics, in background, even in intelligence, determination and achievement, be such opposites? How was it possible for one to have the capacity to feel so much, while the other was incapable of feeling anything?

Aristedes was tugging his wife ahead, to be the

one to meet Naomi first. "Ms. Sinclair, please meet my wife, Selene."

Selene Sarantos was the embodiment of her name. A moon goddess, tall and voluptuous, with a waterfall of ebony silk hair and the most vivid, midnight-blue eyes Naomi had ever seen. But she was more than beautiful, she was…ripened. By the passionate worship of the virile, powerful Aristedes.

Selene extended her hand to Naomi with the smile of someone who had no idea who she was meeting, but was very open to making the new acquaintance. It was clear she didn't mind finding her incredible husband with an unknown woman. That she was okay with that, and with having women like the gorgeous Cora working so close to him, was a testament to her security in his fidelity and her hold over his heart.

Naomi shook her hand with a smile she hoped wasn't brittle. "Pleased to meet you, Mrs. Sarantos."

Selene let out a crystalline laugh. "Selene, please. I'm Mrs. Sarantos everywhere. In private, I want to revert to being Selene only."

"You're *Louvardis*-Sarantos everywhere," Aristedes mock griped.

Selene laughed again, her eyes crinkling at Naomi. "Would you drop a name like Louvardis if you can possibly keep it?"

Naomi shook her head, making the connection. "If you mean Louvardis of Louvardis Enterprises fame, I certainly wouldn't. I wouldn't anyway, based on the chicness and uniqueness of the name alone."

Selene turned her face up to her husband's, her eyes teasing and caressing him, and telling him so, so much. "You see?"

"Oh, I do see." His eyes caressed her back, and Naomi doubted that this was ever an actual issue with him.

Aristedes would be happy with anything that made Selene happy. Keeping her maiden name in combination with his was evidently important to her, maintaining her identity and paying tribute to her father and family. And that was exactly what Aristedes would want her to do.

And *Naomi* had to go fixate on the one man incapable of giving her a look like that, of valuing her or needing her or considering her anywhere near the way Aristedes did Selene...or at all.

The familiar sense of futility twisted her insides again as Aristedes turned to her. "Shall we sit down, Ms. Sinclair?"

"Naomi, please, Mr. Sarantos." He opened his mouth, and she rushed to preempt him. "But please don't expect me to call *you* anything else."

"We'll see, *Ms. Sinclair*," he drawled, renewed shrewdness invading his gaze as they sat down, she in an armchair, he and Selene on the couch. "Once we find out what you want to see me about." After a minute of silence, he added, "Please relax."

A nervous giggle escaped her. "Ms. Delaney advised me the same on the way up here. She assured me I have nothing to fear from you, if only on account of Mrs. Sarantos being here today."

The next moment a gust of wind could have blown her away. She was, anyway. By Aristedes's smile. And what a smile it was. Especially as he turned to share the joke with Selene.

"You sure came at the best time, Ms. Sinclair. Selene is so busy with our kids and her own firm that she rarely visits me at work. Her arrival has me in a celebratory mood, so you'll find me most receptive to whatever you need to say. Though if it's about Andreas, I'm sure I won't like hearing it. But it seems you dislike having to tell it even more. The best way around that is to just spit it out. So let's have it."

Naomi looked uncertainly at Selene.

Aristedes waved. "You can say anything in front of my wife. I'll tell her everything, anyway, and this saves me having to recount it to her later."

Selene gave him a chiding glance, then turned reassuring eyes on her. "You don't have to say anything in front of me. I'll leave if it will make you more comfortable."

Naomi lunged forward and stopped Selene as she rose. "Oh, no, please, stay. I was only uncertain how Mr. Sarantos would prefer this. I would actually like you to stay."

"As a buffer against any crankiness, no doubt." Selene smiled at her, then at her husband as she sat back. He reached for her hand with an answering smile, caressing it as if compelled, clearly finding extreme pleasure and comfort in the action.

The sight of them as they sat unconsciously entwined even as they focused on someone else was exquisite. Two powerful entities who'd come together in a far bigger and stronger new whole. This was more than love. This was…unity.

But every second in their company underlined ever more painfully how stunted Andreas was, how hopeless it had always been with him, and what a terrible future awaited her and Dora if Aristedes couldn't help her.

Drawing in a steadying breath, she told them everything.

They both listened attentively, even if their reactions to her account were diametrically different.

Selene looked increasingly pained, as if imagining herself in Naomi's place, being forced into such an emotionally traumatic choice, with her children's future hanging in the balance. Aristedes only looked progressively more angry. Enraged.

He was evidently a protector, had severe issues with the coercion of anyone weaker, especially a woman. That the one guilty of such a transgression was his brother, the brother he evidently thought very little of, exacerbated his outrage. It was as if it tarnished his own honor that this intimidation was originating from someone who shared his blood.

By the time she finished, Aristedes looked as cold as his brother always did, but she could feel the volcano beneath. It was so scary she almost blurted out a defense of Andreas. But she stopped herself. She couldn't ruin her own petition in order to protect Andreas from his brother's wrath now that she was certain she'd managed to unleash it.

But she only wanted her and Dora's salvation, she didn't want Andreas hurt in the process. Even if he wasn't bothered in the least by the idea of hurting her.

Before she could say anything, Aristedes squeezed Selene's hands, which were now clinging to his, and disengaged from her to rise to his feet. Naomi staggered up to hers, explanations and excuses crowding on her tongue.

Aristedes gave her no chance to voice them, taking her hand in both of his, giving it a reassuring squeeze. "Ms. Sinclair…Naomi…you don't have to worry. Petros was like a younger brother to me back in Crete, to us all. Once he got here, we never reestablished relationships, as his friendship with Andreas took him wherever Andreas was—away from any of us. I can't begin to tell you how much I regret that we didn't know of you all, of his marriage or his death. But now I know of his daughter, I assure you she is as precious to me as any of my nephews and nieces. I would never let anyone disrupt her life, or yours, least of all Andreas. Leave him to me."

After she thanked him and received further bolstering from Selene, Naomi left in a state of imbalance.

All she hoped was that she hadn't set up an impending clash that would lead to an unbridgeable rift between the brothers. Not that they had much of a relationship to preserve, but still. She couldn't bear to think it would be severed totally on her account.

But it was already done. Aristedes would order Andreas to back off, might even pressure him. She doubted Andreas would buckle easily. Or at all. He was too powerful and established, and he didn't care about losses. It was how he'd grown so big. By being fearless and holding nothing dear.

Still, Aristedes was now an ally. He would buy her time, or manage to negotiate terms she could live with. Such as making Andreas take her offer instead of insisting on his terms.

Or it could all go horribly wrong.

Unable to think about the consequences of the events she'd set in motion, she only hoped this would be resolved with the least damage possible. And that she and Dora would be saved from plummeting into Andreas's void.

<u>Six</u>

Andreas stopped in front of the building he'd passed so many times during the past years and never entered. His older brother's office building.

The brother who'd called him an hour ago and ordered him to report to his office. Aristedes's growled "now" was still a dull pain in his left ear.

His first reaction was to tell him what to do with his imperious summons. He *would* have ignored him, if he didn't realize with near certainty what this was all about.

Naomi.

There was no other explanation. Aristedes had called him only four times in as many years. For Leonidas's funeral, for his own wedding, and for their youngest sister's son's first birthday, which had also become her wedding. Andreas had gone only to Caliope's wedding, because the situation had allowed it.

Another major event in the family would be too much of a coincidence a day after Naomi had fled from him, calling him a monster. No, Aristedes's aggressive, out-of-the-blue call had to be at her instigation and on her behalf. She must have thought her last resort was to sic Aristedes on him. Not because he was his older brother. She must know that would have no influence on him. But because he was Aristedes.

Aristedes *was* formidable. If anyone could stand up to Andreas, it would be him. She must have calculated Aristedes would at least slow him down while she kept searching for a way out that didn't include surrender. The wily, fiery lioness.

But she *had* surrendered last night. She'd come to him gloriously furious and taken all her aggression and passion out on him. She'd hit and bit and rubbed against him until he'd given her what she'd come demanding. And it had been as mind-blowing as it had always been. More, as if the time apart had boosted everything they'd shared, the intimacy more searing, the pleasure more excruciating.

But as soon as he'd realized what had driven her into his arms, he'd grown cold. If only for minutes. He'd always been certain Naomi suffered his same affliction. He knew she'd do anything to end up beneath him, as he would to have her there.

She might have a legitimate excuse in Dorothea, but it *had* been only an excuse. She'd wanted him. That was why she'd offered herself to him. Whether for Dorothea or anything else, she certainly would have never gone to another man's bed....

The idea caused an instant boiling in his blood.

A whack against his arm brought the surge of ferocity to a jarring end.

Great. He'd literally gone blind with possessiveness. He'd knocked a man over as he entered the building like a charging bull.

Helping the man to his feet, Andreas apologized, ignoring his curiosity and that of everyone around as he walked into the huge, ultramodern lobby.

It was clear everyone had recognized him, whether as himself or on account of his unmistakable likeness to Aristedes. They must be wondering what tremendous incident could have brought the prodigal brother back.

Last night had been tremendous indeed.

What had happened between them until Naomi had come out of the fugue of passion had been overwhelming. And *real*. What he shared with her was the only thing that he was certain *was* real. The unstoppable chemistry, the explosive satisfaction.

What had she called it? An unhealthy level of sexual affinity? Substituting "unhealthy" for "addictive" and "enslaving" was more like it. Whether that was unhealthy or not, he'd never cared. Not when it was that magnificent.

He'd cared only after she'd left him, when he could no longer wallow in his addiction and enslavement. Through the years, his body had hardened just reliving being buried inside her, his nerves constantly buzzing with the memorized feel of her velvet skin and resilient flesh, his nostrils always filled with echoes of the distillation of her essence and overpowering femininity. Relief, deficient and short-lived, he'd only achieved by replaying their countless encounters of abandon.

After the years of torment, he'd been as angry as Naomi, though for a different reason. At her hold over him. He'd come back intending to reclaim her, but had been hoping it would be different, that he'd be cured of addiction. He'd hoped he'd still be attracted, but not compelled.

But then he had seen her, touched her, and his fever had spiked to its previous power....and exceeded it, too.

Everything about her—the texture of her skin, the sound of her gasps, the melody of her voice, the taste of her kiss, the scent of her breath, the magic of her glances and gestures—it was as if her every nuance was his very own designer drug, a mind-altering high and an aphrodisiac in one, specifically formulated for him by a merciless god of compulsion.

Then had come last night. *Theós*...last night.

He'd thought bingeing on her pleasures would break starvation's hold over his senses. It had only fractured the leash on his cravings. Now they ran rampant, would consume him if he didn't have her again. And a thousand times more.

And there he was, standing in the lobby of one of the busiest buildings on Fifth Avenue, fielding dozens of curious stares and about to tussle with his older brother. And all he could think of was her, beneath him, hot and wet and incoherent with lust, her petal-soft arms clasped around him, her velvet inferno core gripping him as he drove into her, inundating her with pleasure and pouring his seed inside her.

His heart thundered, all blood rushing to his erection, forcing him to come to a full stop.

Dekára. Dammit. He was so hard he'd hurt himself if he moved.

At least being crammed so unbearably in his jeans had an upside. They were tight enough to obscure his arousal. If not according to the stares of the men. They had this male empathy in their eyes acknowledging his predicament, before they looked around to check out who was causing it.

They'd realize his condition was more advanced than it looked if they knew the instigator of his libido crisis not only wasn't around, but had also laid the trap he was walking into.

And he had to walk into it and get it over with, so he could resume her pursuit. He'd go into serious withdrawal soon....

"Mr. Sarantos."

Turning his head, he found a woman rushing toward him. He deflated in the time it took her to reach him.

With a tentative smile, she extended a hand to

him. "Cora Delaney. Mr. Sarantos sent me to escort you to his office without delay."

Giving her a brief handshake, he absently noted how her gaze flickered. He was certain she didn't look at Aristedes that way. Then a slightly wider smile and direct eye contact let him know she was *very* interested, if he was.

Glancing ahead without returning her smile, he started walking, a clear message that he wasn't.

She was pretty. Beautiful, even. Years ago she'd have been his type. Dark and vivid and svelte. He would have let her know his interest was fleeting, to take it or leave it. Once she'd agreed to his terms, he would have let himself be picked up, for an evening.

Then Naomi had happened. A voluptuous angel with sunlight spun in her hair and turquoise shores trapped in her eyes, vulnerable and valiant, innocent and insatiable. And that had been it for him. Ever since, it had been her…or nothing.

Women, on the other hand, remained interested, made advances everywhere he went. Whenever a passive dismissal like the one he'd given Ms. Delaney wasn't enough, he ended the situation by saying he was already taken.

And he was. Naomi had taken his libido prisoner from that first look, a genie in a bottle that only she could unleash.

She was unleashing something else now. Aristedes's wrath. Andreas had better start gearing his mind to that.

As he did, he finally noticed his surroundings. Everything in the building was stamped with Aristedes's character, at least his professional side, austere, oozing with class and power, unflinchingly distinctive and cutting edge.

In minutes, they'd arrived at their destination and Ms. Delaney left him to enter his brother's den alone.

Walking in without slowing down, he crossed what had to be a waiting room, rounded a corner… and saw Aristedes.

He was standing like a monolith in the middle of the expansive room, his reflection in the polished hardwood floor giving the illusion of him rising from another world, like a god of vengeance. He sure looked the part.

Something shifted deep inside Andreas at the sight of his brother. Something elemental. Unreasoning and overpowering.

Because of his choices, he'd never truly known Leonidas, his younger brother. He'd been better with Petros. He hoped. But the feeling of being too late, doing too little for either of them, never stopped creeping up on him and garroting him with regrets. Now they were both gone, so tragically, so prematurely, both to car accidents. Leonidas's had been ruled as his fault, but at least no one else had been hurt by his tragic mistake. Now Aristedes was the only brother Andreas had left. The only *male* in this world who was close to him.

Granted, they were not close in reality, which was also his doing. But there was this fundamental bond, this inexorable tug in his blood that recognized Aristedes's, its kindred nature soothing and bolstering him by its purity and power.

And though said kindred entity was now glaring at him as if he wanted nothing but to flay him, Andreas reached out and pulled him into a hug.

Aristedes went stone still in his embrace, made no move at all, even to breathe. His heart might have stopped. He was that shocked.

Not that Andreas could have expected a different reaction. He'd never showed Aristedes or anyone else any spontaneous demonstration of affection, physical, verbal or otherwise.

Sighing, he stepped away, releasing him. He

didn't want his brother to suffocate or have a heart attack, after all.

Aristedes stared ahead as if in a trance. Then he shook his head as if to exit one, and his vacant gaze panned to Andreas.

"What was that all about?" he rasped.

Andreas shrugged. "I'm almost certain that was what people refer to as a brotherly hug."

"Since when are brotherly hugs applicable to your species, Andreas?"

He gave another shrug, more dismissing. "I felt like it, I did it. Let it go."

"How can I let it go? You *hugged* me, Andreas. This is right up there with…with the sky raining fish."

"I'm sure *that* happened in some historically obscure event. And no doubt won't again. As this hug won't."

"If it happened, then a set of bizarre circumstances came together to make the impossible occur. What happened to make you hug me?"

Exhaling, Andreas pulled Aristedes into another hug, a rougher, briefer one, then pushed him away. "There. I took it back. Or put it back. Or whatever returns you to your former state before the anomaly occurred. Better now?"

"If you think I can be the same, that *anything* can be the same after this, you've got another think coming. What's going on with you, Andreas? Are you...sick?"

A mirthless laugh escaped him. "You think I'm dying or something? And what? I'm overcome with regret for all the things I've missed, all the things I haven't done or said, and I've come to make amends before it's too late?"

His sarcasm was evidently lost on Aristedes, who scanned him in anxiety-tinged exasperation. "*Are* you okay, dammit? If there's something wrong with you, tell me *now.*"

Andreas winced, pressing his hand over the still aching eardrum that his brother's previous "now" had almost ruptured. "It was just a damn hug, Aristedes, and I took it back. What else can I do to restore our peaceful, subzero-expectations status quo?"

The emotions in Aristedes's gaze evaporated, the void Andreas had seen in the mirror for as long as he could remember filling their place.

Andreas had long perfected this unreadable stare as a weapon and a defense mechanism, until it had become a part of him. He lost his grip on it only when he was too stimulated or disturbed. In other words, with Naomi.

Born into the same hell before him, Aristedes had developed his own array of disturbingly blank stares long before life had taught Andreas the need for them. Being an expert in all their brands, he recognized the significance of this one. It was his brother's substitute for putting him over his knee.

After making sure he'd hit him with its full brunt, Aristedes turned and strode to the sitting area.

As soon as Andreas joined him, he said, "Do you want to restore it?"

"Our status quo? You mean we really exited it? We now have Pre-Hug and Post-Hug status quos?"

Another look. "Just. Answer. Do you?"

Did he? What if he didn't? He was so used to his segregation he had no idea if he could handle anything else, or if he was even equipped for it.

Andreas exhaled. "Nothing needs to change."

"I think everything needs to change. *You* need to change."

"And you know that because you're my big brother who knows best?"

"I know that because I *was* you until a few years ago."

"Until Selene came along and saved you from yourself."

It still seemed unreal to Andreas that Aristedes, of all men, had fallen in love, and with the daughter of his worst enemy. Of course, it had started out bumpy and their initial tryst had ended in separation, during which she'd had his baby, but thought he didn't deserve to be told. Once he'd gone back, she'd made him jump through hoops for the privilege of another chance with her and of knowing his son. Being an overachiever, Aristedes had gone overboard proving himself, and would clearly never stop doing so. They were now married, with another child, a daughter, living a happily-ever-after that was far more perfect than any fairy tale.

It was all too nauseating, really.

"Ridiculing it doesn't make it any less true," Aristedes said. "Selene did save me. She dragged every worthwhile thing out of me, and gave me a second and real chance at life."

"Then I'm doomed, since according to you I have no such worthy stuff lurking inside me to be excavated."

"I was as bad as you and worse. Turns out it's not important if *you* think you are worthy of redemption. What's important is that *someone* thinks you are, and you're not too stupid to let them reach out to you."

"You were never as bad as me, Aristedes. I'm in a class of my own, remember?" He shook his head. "I can't believe the conversation we're having. And over a hug, too. It's not as if this was the first time I hugged you."

"The last time you hugged me you were seven, Andreas."

"Ne." Thirty years ago.

He looked away, and into the past. He remembered how he'd felt about Aristedes then. His brother had been his anchor, the only beacon of hope and strength in a dark and turbulent existence. He'd loved his mother and older sisters, as a child would those who cared for him. But he'd recognized them as fellow victims, to be despised for their helplessness just as he'd despised himself. It was only Aristedes he'd admired, whose determination had set his own course, whose drive had imbued him with the will to fight.

Andreas exhaled. "I never told you, but I idolized the hell out of you back then. You were my role model."

"That I believe. Your role model in detachment. But in my case it was a tool, what I needed to survive, then to get ahead. For you, it seems to be a fundamental component. Or rather, the absence of one. It seems the entity responsible for putting you together in the cosmic factory left your emotional package on the conveyor belt."

"You are the second one in as many days to tell me I lack such an essential building block. I can only be grateful for its absence, since I can't imagine what it would have been like having it when I was around our father. Or the other pieces of shit who littered my path. I would have wasted so much time and energy *feeling* stuff about them when they're not worth a second thought. *You,* on the other hand, always warranted an actual response from me."

"I never had any idea you even noticed I was alive. Not when you looked at me with the same lack of concern you bestowed on everything and everyone else."

"Oh, I noticed you, and looked up to you…when you were around to be looked up to."

Aristedes frowned, as if in remembered pain. "You know I couldn't be around when I had to provide for you all."

Andreas waved away his justification. "I was there, remember?"

And he'd been there in a way Aristedes had no idea about. When his brother was working twenty-hour days to put food on the table, Andreas had been left behind, the "man of the house." And the things he'd had to do to fill that role...

"Is this about Petros?"

Andreas blinked at Aristedes's question, Petros's name skewering his heart.

"I always thought you felt nothing for anyone except Petros. His death, though you didn't deem to inform us of it, must have hit you hard, even if you wouldn't admit it."

"Why wouldn't I? I admit it. I'm still reeling."

It was Aristedes's turn to blink in surprise at the ready admission. "You are? I mean, it's only natural anyone would be, but it's just that you are..."

"Not natural? Probably. But he was as close to me as anyone ever was. Closer than any of you."

"Which wouldn't be saying much, since you weren't close to any of us in any way. It seemed you turned thirteen and just...shut down, turned away from everyone."

"This, coming from the man who gave his family money and services in lieu of human interaction. Mother used to say you sold your soul for a Midas touch. And speaking of hugs, she said she'd gladly exchange everything you gave her for one hug."

Aristedes's frown turned thunderous. "We're

not discussing which of us was the colder bastard, Andreas."

Andreas grimaced. "*Theos*...listen, I'm sorry. That was a cheap shot. Too cheap. I didn't condone what she said or felt. In fact, I actually despised her for it. You supported us in an impossible situation, then got us all out of Crete, made us new lives in the States, which she didn't live to see because she killed herself with a broken heart over our scum-of-the-earth father. Our mother was sick, with toxic emotionalism that caused her to make every wrong choice possible, and scarred us all for life. She worshiped our father, who told her sweet lies while he swindled her out of her whole life, and she didn't appreciate the miracles you were achieving for all of us, because you didn't do them with a smile and a hug. Is it any wonder we grew up despising such poisonous sentimentalities?"

Aristedes's gaze sharpened, as if he was viewing their lives in a new light, seeing Andreas from an unexpected angle.

At last he said, "Our mother was damaged, for too many reasons, as was our father, and their relationship was pathological. But we left them and their legacy far behind, and shouldn't let their mistakes and shortcomings poison *our* inclinations.

You don't need to go that far in the opposite direction to having no emotions, because you saw what losing herself to them did to her. There is a huge range of balanced feelings you can experience without having them overpower you."

"Like those you feel for Selene and your kids? I think you're way beyond overpowered by those."

"And that's bad only if such emotions are damaging or degrading or depressing. My feelings for Selene and our children resuscitated me and now sustain and rejuvenate me." Aristedes suddenly gave a growl of impatience. "You've taken us on another tangent."

"It's you who started reminiscing about my shutdown."

"What I asked," Aristedes barked, "was if your strange behavior is on account of Petros's loss—"

"I'll never hear the end of this hug, will I?" Andreas interrupted. "Next I'll find Caliope texting me to discuss my unfurling emotional potential." He sat forward, the idea actually making him anxious. Caliope had been trying to reel him into the family circle since he'd made the mistake of attending her wedding. "Whatever you do, *don't* tell Caliope about this. I'll do anything if you promise not to."

"How about you leave Naomi alone?"

So. Moment of truth. The point of all this.

Andreas sat back, cocked his head at his brother. "So she enlisted your services in deterring me, eh? What did she tell you? I should hear her list of charges before we go on."

And for the next ten minutes, Aristedes let him hear, in very colorful language, his own version of Naomi's "charges" and what he thought of him and his actions.

His rebukes were still echoing like rolling thunder when Andreas finally inhaled. "You done?"

"Yes, and so are you, *agóri*," Aristedes growled.

He huffed. "Been a while since anyone called me boy."

"Don't make me demonstrate that in comparison to me, you *are* still a boy."

"We're comparing sizes now?"

Aristedes sat forward. Andreas was certain any other man would have cowered. "You *will* leave Naomi alone. And that's my last word."

"I wasn't aware this was a bid. But here's *my* last word, so we can wrap this up. There's no way in hell I'm doing that."

"Andreas—"

His raised hand interrupted Aristedes's threat.

"I spent the past four years thinking of nothing but getting her back, and now that I can have her again, I'm not letting her go."

"You'd use your friend's will and his baby to coerce her back into your bed? You care nothing about the fact that she doesn't want to be with you again?"

"She wants nothing more. Trust me on that."

"I trust her word…and the turmoil I saw and felt in her. If you think she wants you, and that's how you're justifying this to yourself, you're self-deluding."

"You know nothing about our history, Aristedes."

"I know everything. She told me."

That surprised him. And intrigued him. He hadn't thought she'd go that far. But what had she said, exactly, to get Aristedes within a hairbreadth of getting physical?

"It might be impossible for you to consider anyone but yourself," his brother said, keeping his temper under control with obvious effort. "But consider this. This is a woman who recently lost her only sister and is still barely dealing with the loss. She inherited the responsibility of her niece—"

"Which she won't shoulder alone when she re-marries me."

"She *didn't* ask for help, least of all yours. I get the impression Dora is all she lives for."

"Which isn't right. Her life shouldn't revolve around the child. That's bad for both of them."

"And what's good? You? The man who failed to give Naomi the minimum of consideration and re-spect in your so-called sham of a marriage? You want to force more heartache on her by holding her daughter hostage? And Dora *is* her daughter in all the ways that count. Are you so without feel-ings or honor?"

"I'll do what I have to do. Wouldn't you do any-thing to get Selene back if you ever lost her?"

"I would never coerce Selene and override her choices like you're doing to Naomi."

"I'm not coercing her, I'm pursuing her. She needs me to, before she can allow herself to do what she really wants to do, which is come back to me."

Aristedes's look was incredulous. "You think she's playing hard to get?"

"Not exactly. It seems she's ashamed that she pursued me in the past. And it seems she took particular exception that I kept our marriage a secret from you all. I believe that's one of the main reasons she came to you, to right this wrong retroactively. I'm restoring her dignity by pursuing her this time. And if she hadn't preempted me, I would have told you about us the moment I got her to agree. So no, I'm not coercing her, I'm giving her the tussle she needs so she can have whatever pound of flesh she feels I owe her. But her reasons for resisting me don't include not wanting me. She does want me, as much as I want her. *Do* trust me on this."

Aristedes got the implication this time—that Andreas had obtained unquestionable proof of his claim, very recently.

Aristedes still plowed on. "You're talking about physical lust, and that's never enough to overcome mental and emotional aversion. If you manage to make her remarry you, a woman who can't bear you out of bed, what do you think you'll do when you're not making love? What kind of dysfunctional battlefield would you have dragged her onto?"

Andreas waved as if to swat away his brother's concerns. "This initial conflict will end soon."

"What if it doesn't? According to her it will only escalate. You'd risk that kind of personal and domestic hell? Just because you want to get her out of your system?"

"I *can't* get her out of my system. And I don't want to."

"That's still just sex."

A mirthless laugh escaped Andreas as he remembered Naomi's exact words last night. And his response. *Just sex, indeed.*

Aristedes went on. "And for that, the arrangement she suggested is the perfect catharsis for both of you."

"I don't want 'an arrangement.' I want a permanent situation."

"Do you even have a concept what permanence is, Andreas? The only pseudo relationship you ever had was with her. You think that's what marriage is? That farce you're asking her to repeat? Even if you're completely detached from the way other people experience emotions, you never waste time on something that doesn't work. Why are you insisting on repeating what failed as absolutely as your first so-called marriage did?"

"I don't think it failed."

"Sure, because divorce is an indication a marriage was a resounding success."

"It indicates…a problem. She must have told you

about it. It doesn't apply anymore, so it won't be the same this time."

Aristedes's growl would have made anyone else run for cover. "Why don't you admit you're after her because she dared to walk away? I wouldn't put it past you that you'd make her bow to your will, only so you'd be the one to walk out, in your own good time."

"I see you've adopted her analysis of my actions and motivations."

"It does suit what I know about you."

Andreas pushed himself to his feet. He'd had enough of this. "I'm done. I won't repeat myself."

Aristedes stood and grabbed his shoulder. "Even if I adopt *your* analysis, you'd still be tussling with her in another passionate if pathological relationship. I might have sanctioned this if it was about the two of you alone. But it isn't. There's a child involved. Didn't you think of that little girl at all? If you get Naomi back in this dishonorable way, life between you will be an even worse hell than it was, and Dora will be caught in the middle."

Andreas frowned. "Who said life between us was hell?"

Aristedes huffed in ridicule. "Naomi, of course."

"It *wasn't* hell," he hissed. "And it wouldn't be."

"That's your word and prediction against hers. And even if you're right, what happens when you get enough of Naomi? Did you think how Dora will feel when you toss her aside along with Naomi after she comes to consider you her father?"

He hadn't thought of any such possibility, since it would never happen. He'd never get enough of Naomi. And he'd never toss Petros's child aside.

But that wasn't what he objected to in Aristedes's conjecture. "I will make it clear to Dorothea from the start that I'm not her father. I have no illusions I could be that."

The flare of disgust in Aristedes's eyes hit him harder than a punch. "I always knew you were cold, but I never dreamed you were heartless." He grasped his arm roughly. "I warn you, Andreas, pursue this and I will stop you, no matter how much I have to damage you to make you back off."

He held his brother's gaze. "You done now?" Aristedes's hand tightened. Andreas removed it with utmost calmness. "Here's how it will be. I will fulfill Petros's will. He wanted Dorothea to be a Sarantos, and that's what I'm making her. I want to make Naomi my wife again, and that is what she'll become."

"Andreas—"

He raised both hands to stem his brother's explosion. "*If* during this process you have any indication that any of Naomi's fears are coming to pass, that I am harming either of them, you can use any deterrent you see fit."

"You think I'll wait until you cause them harm?"

"Why are you so certain I will? Aren't you the advocate of second chances? Didn't you just lecture me on redemption? Or do you believe those are possible for everyone else but me?"

Uncertainty entered Aristedes's eyes and his aggression dissipated in the span of a heartbeat. "If I thought for a moment this is what you're after..."

Andreas reached a hand to his brother's shoulder, held it and his gaze with his pledge. "It is."

An hour later, sitting on the bed where he'd taken Naomi last night, Andreas closed his eyes and let the echoes of the magnificence they'd shared reverberate inside him.

Groaning, he fell back among the covers she'd wrapped around her hot, fragrant body, turned his face to inhale deeper her bouquet, letting her lingering scent and sensuality cloak him.

His arousal had been so hair-trigger after she'd left, he'd dragged himself off to sleep in another room. He was still in agony, but his other distur-bance was canceling the worst of it.

This disturbance had nothing to do with his meeting with Aristedes. In fact, he felt...con-tented that they'd had that confrontation. Even if his brother had spent 90 percent of the time scold-ing him like the father he'd—*they'd*—never had, and expressing his disappointment in him, it had only...pleased him. More than that. It had appeased him.

Amid all the disapproval and dressing-down, one thing had become clear. One thing he hadn't thought possible. Aristedes cared.

While his brother had become the epitome of caring in his private life, remaining a bulldozer only professionally, Andreas had never thought that this thawing would extend to him. Not when he'd done everything to warrant being frozen out for good.

Not that Aristedes had cut him any slack. He'd pledged to hurt Andreas, badly, if his alleged second-chance bid showed a hint of exploitative cracks.

But far from being bothered by Aristedes's threats, he was actually amused by his father-bear tactics, even warmed that Naomi and Dorothea now had yet another fierce protector. Besides, Aristedes couldn't hurt him. He couldn't be hurt. There'd been one way he could be, and *that* he'd finally resolved.

What disturbed him was what Naomi had told Aristedes. That their marriage had been hell. True, she'd told him that she'd never been more miserable than when she'd been with him. But initially he'd dismissed that statement, thinking she'd made it out of spite, in the heat of the moment. He'd always believed that their marriage, while unorthodox, had been fantastic. Well, as fantastic as possible given the constraints he'd placed on it. Things between them had gone smoothly in general, and explosively in bed—up till that night he'd told her he never wanted children. That had been the established reason he'd believed she'd left him. She had asked for a divorce the very next day, after all.

Now he was no longer sure.

His head told him she'd made those claims of misery to him to make him back off, then to Aristedes to ignite his protectiveness. If said claims weren't total fabrications, she'd probably worked herself up into believing she'd been unhappy with him all along. She could have resented him retroactively for not having a child of her own, something he'd intended to deprive her of as long as she remained with him. Resentment had a way of warping memories and rewriting history.

But his senses told him a different story. Her fierce resistance to any commitment again, even after their mind-melting lovemaking, had felt too real, too distraught. Now he replayed everything she'd said, the way she'd looked and sounded.... Could it be that had been how she'd really felt at the time, not something she'd constructed after the fact?

He'd be the first to admit their relationship had been irregular. When he'd asked her to marry him, he'd wanted a continuation on the same terms of their affair, only with the assurance that he was hers, and that it wouldn't end. He'd thought that would resolve her discontent and uncertainty, since he'd believed her need for permanence and exclusivity had been why she'd walked out in the first place.

He'd known he wasn't husband material in the accepted ways, and his life situation couldn't have accommodated anything different from what he'd offered her. But he'd thought she'd been content with what they shared, that their passion compensated for anything that had been missing. He'd never suspected she'd been unhappy with him, let alone miserable.

It had been why he'd clung so hard when she'd walked away, believing she'd come back to negotiate her needs. Once she did, he'd intended to argue that they had plenty of time before children became an issue, counting on their phenomenal sex life to satisfy her for years before that maternal need became pressing.

But if their sex life had only made her feel worse about herself for putting up with a situation she'd found so awful, what had made her stay that long? And if expecting the same unhappiness was why she was so adamant about not remarrying him, what could he do now?

He *could* coerce her. Easily.

But he wouldn't. It would defeat his purpose. He wanted—*needed* her unpressured eagerness again.

To get that, she had to agree to his proposal of her own free will. But how could he achieve that?

He'd come back believing that Naomi's need for a child had already been fulfilled, eliminating the one obstacle in the way of her return to him. But it seemed she'd needed things from him beside children, things he hadn't been able to give her. And though his situation had changed, he had no idea if he could.

What if he didn't have it in him?

What if Aristedes was right in distrusting him, and the best thing for her, and for Dorothea, was for him to leave them alone? If so, could he do it?

Could he walk away? Forever this time?

Seven

Naomi stared at the schematics on her laptop screen.

They could have been alien runes for all the sense they made to her.

Not that there was anything wrong with them. It was the perpetual shortage of oxygen to her brain that was causing the malfunction. She'd been bating her breath to find out if Aristedes had succeeded in his mission. But he'd told her only that he'd confronted Andreas, and that things were under control. What *that* meant, she had no idea.

Only one thing would make her breathe easy. For Andreas to say he'd forget about Petros's will. Or at least that he'd negotiate a middle ground. Maybe that when Naomi officially adopted Dora, he'd be her godfather...or something.

And that she didn't have to remarry him.

Whenever she'd come to that part, voices inside her kept adding feverishly that he would instead take her up on her offer of unlimited sexual services.

She hadn't had much luck stifling those.

But for three days after Aristedes had summoned his brother, there'd been absolute silence on Andreas's part. No news didn't feel like good news. Not knowing was driving her insane.

She was also suffering from another problem.

Her body, which he'd savagely reawakened, had been tormenting her. It wasn't leaving her a waking or sleeping moment without demanding his.

Turning off her laptop with a huff of exasperation, she snatched her purse and headed out of her office. No use trying to work when she could barely sit or think straight.

Fifteen minutes later she was entering her apartment, to hear Dora's usual jabbering issuing from the family room. The adorable sounds wrung a smile from her tight lips.

Halfway there, she felt as if she'd bumped into

an invisible wall when she heard what emanated from her destination. A deep, deep voice.

Swallowing the heart that seemed to have vaulted into her throat, she forced herself to continue on shaking legs. It might be Aristedes. It probably was. He'd said he'd come to meet Dora, and she'd told him to drop by whenever he could, no advance call necessary. He did sound a lot like Andreas. From a distance their voices could be mistaken for—

She groaned. Who was she fooling? That dark baritone thrummed her already inflamed nerves, itched behind her breastbone and pooled in her loins. Even if her ears and brain couldn't make a positive ID, the rest of her body knew.

That *was* Andreas.

He was here. Uninvited and unannounced again. And with Dora.

Naomi shook off the initial surge of fright. After all, he was still here, hadn't absconded with Dora.

But she'd left herself wide open to his incursion again. She should have made it clear to Hannah that he wasn't welcome here. Should have left strict instructions with the concierge to bar his entrance.

Reaching the family room, she scoped out the situation before making an entrance, no expectations forming in her mind. What she saw sent her thundering heart sputtering.

Andreas was sitting on the couch, looking even more vital than usual in a light beige suit that made his hair and skin glow in contrast. Her cats flanked his sides, Hannah was sitting across from him in the armchair, and Dora played at his feet.

To anyone looking in on the scene, it would have appeared as though this huge man who dwarfed his companions and darkened the whole room was a regular guest here. Hannah seemed so pleased and animated as she talked to him, Loki and Thor were grooming themselves in utmost relaxation, and Dora was handing him her prized toys to inspect, babbling her brand of baby explanations and inquiries nonstop. They all behaved as if being with him was an accustomed and favorite pastime.

And while he looked totally out of place in this scene of domesticity, his demeanor as he matter-of-factly accepted the attention and familiarity her household extended him, belied the fact that this was an unprecedented situation in his experience, and one alien to his nature.

Which mattered not at all right now. The need to charge in, grab Dora and Hannah and get them the hell away from Andreas was so fierce it paralyzed Naomi.

Which was a good thing. She couldn't expose the reality of the situation to Hannah or Dora. Inertia was giving her the chance to get herself together before she walked in.

One other thing held her back: the fact that Andreas knew she was there. The way he lowered his lashes as his eyes shifted in her direction made her certain. He'd always had an uncanny radar where she was concerned. She bet he wasn't acknowledging her presence on purpose. To goad her into some uncalculated response. One she wasn't giving him, even though she felt his magnetic pull tugging at her every instinct and craving.

Cursing under her breath, she straightened and walked into the room.

As soon as she did, Andreas inched to the edge of the couch, still holding Dora's latest offerings, his gaze opaque as usual. Her body nearly roared its demand for his. Having him within reach was sending it bucking like a wild horse against the reins of decorum and prudence.

Gritting her teeth against the hammering urges, she dragged her gaze to Hannah, who was rising with a bright smile.

"Darling, you're home early! Everything all right?"

Failing to return her smile, Naomi felt her heat rising with each step she took closer to Andreas. "Just wrapped things up earlier than expected."

"Great. Now Mr. Sarantos won't have to put up with our company for as long as he'd resigned himself to."

"It's I who had my doubts you'd bear my company that long, Mrs. McCarthy." Andreas's calm self-denunciation dragged Naomi's gaze back to him. She found him looking at Hannah. "And again, it's Andreas. Every time you say Mr. Sarantos I have the urge to look around for my older brother."

"But you must be used to being called Mr. Sarantos, too!"

"I've been suffering this condition since I came back on his turf. New York can't handle more than one Mr. Sarantos, and that's definitely him around here."

Hannah chuckled. "Fine, but only if you call me Hannah."

"That's a relief…Hannah."

And there Hannah went, totally submerged under Andreas's spell.

His gaze turned to Naomi, and suddenly her clothes felt like sandpaper against her skin, and the air felt like the blast of a furnace.

His cool appraisal made it all worse. "In case you're preparing another rebuke for my being here uninvited again, this time I thought you'd be here when I showed up on your doorstep."

As if he didn't know she worked afternoons on Saturdays.

"You could have called ahead." Her attempt at a smile was all for Hannah's sake. "Saved yourself the wait."

"If I did, I wouldn't have had the chance to sample the fantastic walnut-and-spice cake Hannah had just baked when I arrived. And I wouldn't have met the rest of your household."

He turned his gaze to those who'd come to welcome her. Loki and Thor were rubbing against her legs, while Dora clasped her knees, asking to be picked up.

Feeling she'd keel over if she bent too quickly, Naomi petted her cats, then swung Dora up, moving away from Andreas for some breathable air.

She still couldn't stop watching him as he took in the sight of her and Dora smooching each other, his gaze enigmatic and heavy-lidded. She'd never seen this specific look in his eyes before. And it elicited a whole new level of disturbance.

"You must be hungry."

His remark set off firecrackers in her blood. He should know. But she also knew he wasn't making an innuendo. Though he was terminally blunt, he wasn't blatant. Being so came with the need to provoke people, and Andreas didn't consider others at all. And though he'd been provoking her of late, she doubted he'd make a lewd remark in front of Hannah. Those weren't his style, anyway.

"Hannah said you come home famished," he elaborated. "Since you don't eat or snack at work."

Putting Dora down when she squirmed, Naomi shook her head. "I'm not today."

Because I'm only famished for a juggernaut with a body made for sin and a touch that turns me into a mindless mess.

"Which is a relief," Hannah said. "I forgot all about starting dinner, what with Andreas's entertaining company."

Naomi blinked at her. Andreas? *Entertaining* company?

Hannah pulled herself energetically to her feet. "But no matter. Dinner will be ready in half an hour." She turned to him, eyes hopeful. "And of course you're staying?"

"On one condition."

Sure. Andreas always had one. Something that entailed soul forfeiting.

"I won't sit here waiting to be served. I'm simply incapable of being waited on."

Naomi couldn't accuse him of telling a lie here. Andreas was self-sufficient to the point of aggravation. Though they'd always had room service or catering when they'd been together, he'd never let her as much as serve that food. He'd never even let her make him a cup of coffee. Nor had he ever offered to make her one, either.

"So what did you have in mind for dinner, Hannah?" he asked.

"Oh, just baked salmon, mashed potatoes and stir-fry. The crème brûlée for dessert is ready. But I can put together another menu if any of this isn't to your liking."

"You just mentioned some of my favorite foods."

He wasn't being polite, as he never bothered to be. This was true.

He rose, falling in step with Hannah on her way to the kitchen. She was clearly overjoyed to have him, touching him the way she did David, her only son among her four children, whenever he came visiting. The rest of Naomi's "household" followed in his wake, cats twining between his legs and Dora determinedly crawling after him.

And since she hadn't even been consulted in his dinner invitation, and unable to make a scene in the others' presence, Naomi grudgingly followed.

Once in the kitchen, Dora climbed his leg, demanding he be the one to put her in her high chair. He looked down at her as if one of the cats had started talking to him.

Expecting him to ignore her, Naomi was surprised when he bent and, with perfect efficiency devoid of an emotional element, did as asked. Seemingly satisfied with his handling, Dora pointed to her feeding-time toys that were lined on the marble island. He didn't comply this time, just pinned her with one of his mesmerizing glances. In a moment, the baby's face scrunched up in its most endearing expression.

Naomi couldn't believe it. This was Dora asking nicely!

Only then did Andreas give her what she wanted. Then he bent and looked her straight in the eyes. "And *now* I cook with your mommy and nanny. *You* play until we're done."

Naomi bet Dora understood his refusal to be at her disposal when he had other things to do, and that it was nonnegotiable. Giving him another wide grin, she got busy with her toys.

He moved next to Hannah. "I'll take care of that salmon. I think you'll be impressed with my seasoning."

With a smile that split her face, Hannah offered him the fish and all the ingredients he asked for.

Shaking herself out of the trance she'd fallen into at the impossible sight of Andreas in her kitchen, sharing dinner preparation, Naomi said, "I'll do the potatoes."

Andreas extended her one of those multi-meaning glances before turning his attention to his chore. "That's a perfect cut of salmon. Kudos to whoever chose it. And you must have felt I'd be coming, Hannah, since there's enough for all of us. For Dorothea, too, if she eats that kind of food now."

Glowing from his praise, the older woman said, "Dora eats most of what we eat. She is the least fussy eater of all the babies I've ever dealt with, and I've dealt with six beside her."

"Naomi was one of those, I hear. How was she?"

Hannah looked at her apologetically. "From one

to ten, one being Dora? She was an eleven. Nothing pleased her, and it was over two years before we managed to get her to eat anything not specifically prepared for her."

"I eat anything you put before me now, Hannah."

At her mumbled response, Hannah smiled lovingly at her. "Oh, you've long made up and then some, in every way possible, for any aggravation you ever caused."

Andreas's eyes were on her, contemplative. It must be difficult for him to imagine her being particular about anything. She'd bet she'd been the most accommodating person he'd ever known. Life had punched and wrung any demanding tendencies and expectations out of her.

After he removed the salmon skin, he spoke again. "I grew up on Crete, and most of our food was seafood we caught ourselves, but we never had salmon, since it doesn't exist in the Mediterranean. Once I was introduced to it here, I got addicted. I now eat no other animal protein."

"Is it a moral or health stance?" Hannah asked.

"I can't claim either, no. We could never afford meat or poultry. And when I tried them for the first time here, at age sixteen, I just couldn't develop a taste for them."

Naomi's hands shook as she peeled the potatoes. She'd noticed he'd never eaten those things, but had never asked why. He'd never given her straight answers to anything, so she'd stopped asking. But there he was, volunteering information about his past for the first time.

She'd known, from Aristedes's background and from Andreas's slight Greek accent, that he'd spent his formative years in Crete. She'd had no idea exactly when he'd come to the States. Now she knew. And that they'd been *that* destitute. That must have entailed endless difficulties and uncertainties.

It was impossible to imagine Andreas as a boy, poor and powerless. But maybe that had been responsible for turning him into this self-contained, invulnerable entity.

She suppressed a wave of sympathy with all she had, kept her distance as she prepared her part of the meal. He didn't try to invade her space, either. He took no opportunity to brush against her or touch her, though as they moved around the kitchen, there were plenty of those. Every time one presented itself, she held her breath, every nerve ending in a rage of anticipation. But he took advantage of none.

Even though his aloofness kept pushing her frustration higher, she was amazed at how easily and efficiently they worked together. It was as if they did this every day.

When the meal was ready, he set the table while she fed Dora and Hannah cleaned up. They sat down in the kitchen, as he'd insisted on observing their everyday practices.

Naomi sampled the salmon and was once again amazed. It was the best she'd ever had. His seasoning brought out the fish's natural taste, and made her eager for the next bite of complex and incredible flavors. When she and Hannah said so, he merely accepted their praise, without a show of either pleasure or modesty. He *knew* he was good.

He had to be superlative in everything, didn't he?

But what flabbergasted Naomi was that he was entertaining.

Now that he was actually talking, and not only brooding and distilling his responses to absolute minimums, he was witty, sometimes even funny. The strangeness of the situation was the only thing that kept her from engaging him fully, from demonstrating the effect his wit and drollness had on her.

At one point, as he related anecdotes about his early childhood, he said, "I barely saw my father, growing up, and I considered Aristedes an entity unto himself, whom I didn't consider in the simple terms of a male or female role model. My brother Leonidas was still a work-in-progress at the time. Then one day I demanded a dress like my sisters. I felt discriminated against, wearing only shorts and pants. It was only then that my mother broke the news that I couldn't wear a dress because I was a boy. You can't imagine my shock at that disclosure."

Naomi couldn't hold back anymore; she burst out laughing.

For this overwhelmingly masculine man to be sitting here admitting he'd thought he was a girl, had been happy thinking it, and crestfallen when he'd found out the truth, was just...hilarious.

He slanted her a long-suffering glance. "Go ahead and laugh. My sisters howled for days. And with every stage I passed through after that earth-shaking revelation, their amusement escalated."

"What stages were those?" she spluttered.

"The usual. Denial, then anger then bargaining..."

She snorted. "Bargaining?"

"I was certain there must be something that could be done to stop this condition in its tracks, or to reverse it." At her renewed peals of laughter he sighed in mock despair. "You can laugh now, but I was grief-stricken. I felt so betrayed when I found out this condition was permanent."

Thankfully, for her. Or maybe not so thankfully. His overriding maleness had cost her six years, and would probably be *the* source of torment for the rest of her life.

But even this thought couldn't dampen her mirth right now. "You must have been very young."

"Six. It took me a year to accept my terrible fate."

After that, the conversation flowed, so spontaneously, so enjoyably. Hannah made few contributions, watching them with evident pleasure and keeping Dora entertained all through the meal.

It felt so natural having him there, talking to him that way, that Naomi had to keep reminding herself this was indeed Andreas, the man who'd shut her out all through their relationship, who'd never showed her any of the ease and unaffectedness he offered so freely now. By the end of the meal, it was difficult to accept that her dinner companion and that other Andreas were one and the same man.

Was this the real him? If so, what had kept

this wonderful person locked up in ice all these years? What had happened now to thaw him out? It couldn't be her, since she'd never succeeded in unleashing these facets of him before.

But being exposed to said facets only caused her condition to worsen. She had to fight the urge to drag his hands to her burning cheeks or aching breasts, or to lean into him and rest her head on his chest. From the look in his eyes, she surmised that he saw it all—and chose not to respond with the merest touch or even an acknowledgment.

After a brief lull as Hannah rose to fetch dessert, Naomi said, "I thought you left town."

This came out too much like an accusation for her liking.

But the contrary emotions he wrung from her were tearing her in two opposite directions. She did want him to leave. For Dora's sake. But when she'd thought he'd left without a word, after the night they'd had, the thought had been a hot poker in her middle.

He thanked Hannah as she placed his crème brûlée in front of him, then said, "I'm here to stay…for a while."

Conscious of Hannah's piqued attention, Naomi emptied her voice of expression. "For how long?"

"It depends."

"On what?"

"On when I'll conclude the business I have here."

"What if you don't, or can't?"

One formidable shoulder rose in an indolent shrug. "I'll deal with the possibilities as they arise. My plans are fluid."

Just as her insides were, being this close to him.

After that, she let him draw her back into their bantering, though it was more difficult to keep up her end, since thoughts of him leaving and her fluid-with-desire state had put a damper on her mood.

Then they moved back to the family room for coffee.

The cats rushed to climb on his lap as soon as he sat down, but Dora insisted on evicting and replacing them. Since they considered her the baby of the family, while they were old and wise felines, they moved on, in obvious displeasure. They didn't go far, though, and sat flanking him again, grooming the fur messed by the tussle with Dora.

Andreas let the baby explore him, not helping or hindering her. Soon she made it impossible for him to continue his conversation with Naomi, demanding his attention by grabbing for his phone, belt buckle and anything he held. She whined when he refused to bow to her will.

He did that without a trace of irritation. Naomi wondered how, since Dora was being *very* irritating. Which was probably a good thing, she reasoned, since it would give him a taste of what it would be like if he took on responsibility for her, even if not as her main caretaker.

But if he showed no irritation, neither did he exhibit any indulgence, not in the way he regarded Dora, not in his refusal to let her use him and his articles for her new take-apart or teething toys.

At Dora's latest antic, trying to find out if the silky bronze hair on his chest was attached, things took a turn for the confrontational.

When he stopped her, if not gently, at least carefully, the baby's lip curled downward.

"You're a demanding little tyke, aren't you?"

For good measure, Dora's chin shook and her eyes filled with tears.

"And a grade A manipulator, too."

Dora lunged again at his open shirt in pursuit of her interrupted experiment, making Naomi rush to take her away.

Andreas raised a hand, staying her movement. Sitting back down, she itched to end this, since

Dora began to sob with frustration as he held her chubby little hands at bay. Short of snatching her from him, and making this even worse, there was nothing Naomi could do but wait and see how he would handle it. She had no hope it would be in any way suited to a baby.

With both of them ignoring her presence completely, they locked horns, Dora's eyes indignant and swimming in tears of frustration, his contemplative yet unyielding.

Then in a very quiet voice, as if he was whispering in confidence, he said, "Here's how it will be, Dorothea. These are my hairs, and they stay on my chest. You don't get to feel bad about not getting something you shouldn't ask for. But I promise, when you want something you can have, I'll let you have it. How about that?"

And wonder of wonders, the willful, tearful expression on Dora's face dissipated as he calmly discussed the situation with her as he would with an adult. Then, seeming to accept his nonnegotiable terms, she gave a yell of glee, as if she hadn't been agitated a moment ago, and threw herself on the chest she'd been keen on attacking, and rubbed her face in it. Andreas made no attempt to hug her, as anyone else would have. Which didn't deter Dora in the least. Moments later, she raised her head with a smile that Naomi could swear was deferential, then she scrambled off him and went about her business.

Although the situation had been calmly resolved without her intervention, Naomi felt compelled to say something.

"Sorry about that. She's not usually so demanding. It must be the novelty of having someone other than Hannah and me around. And a man, at that."

His gaze acknowledged that the one man who'd been a constant presence in her life, Petros, had been taken from her when she'd been too young. She had either forgotten him or hadn't really formed any memories of him.

Andreas's eyes grew thoughtful. "She doesn't see any men?"

"None like you."

He made no comment on that, her placing him in a category of his own, but his stare made Naomi's every cell start to sizzle like popcorn.

To break the tension she muttered, "I guess she was exploring her boundaries with you, since you're a new and totally different person. She already knows her boundaries with us."

"Are you sure she has any? You and Hannah anticipate all her needs and whims. That's the reason she's undemanding. You leave her nothing to demand."

"Are you saying we're overindulging her?"

"Claws back into your paws, mother lioness. I'm not criticizing your upbringing methods, I'm observing. As someone new around here, I might be able to see what you can't, because you're too used to the dynamics in your family and too settled in its rules. But I do think there's a definite risk of overindulgence here. If only from her growing up realizing she's the center of your and Hannah's universe."

"I'm sure you have a suggestion how to rectify this."

"None. It must be next to impossible to look at someone this size, someone so totally dependent on you, and be objective. Considering the situation, too, it's understandable you're trying to compensate her, and perhaps ending up overcompensating."

"So what you're really saying is that I'm a bad mother."

She was expecting him to say "you're not a mother at all" or something to that effect, but he again surprised her. "I have no idea what kind of mother you are, Naomi. I've been here a few hours and Dorothea spent those focusing on me. I had only fleeting impressions of your relationship—which could turn out to be totally off the mark on closer inspection. But I expect you'd be as efficient in this role as you are in everything else. I'm only wondering if your overachieving tendencies might not be best applied in this field."

"*I'm* an overachiever?"

"You most definitely are, and that is something to be proud of. In your professional life. With Dorothea, on the other hand, it could lead to…"

"…overindulging her."

"It's likely, and it would be understandable. That said, if you say she's undemanding in general, I'll take your word for it. She did respond promptly to my refusal to indulge her whim, after all."

Naomi bit her tongue so she wouldn't admit that it was his handling and influence that had resolved the situation so amicably, not the baby's responsiveness.

Still, she felt the urge to explain Dora's character more. "She is overly inquisitive sometimes, but it's not whims that make her demanding. She just gets very interested in things, in how they work, what they're made of. Demanding brats often lose interest as soon as you give them what they fussed for. But once you give Dora what she asked for, she sits aside and examines it for hours. All her favorite toys are articles from around the house that she demanded, and she never lost interest in them. In fact, she keeps finding new uses for them, alone or together."

"Seems we have an inventor on our hands. But it's too bad she got interested in things I couldn't let her have. My phone and belt *could* have been negotiated, but my chest hair…that would have to remain taboo."

Naomi's smile broke out, wiping away her defensive tension. Though he didn't smile back, there was an unknown warmth in his eyes that felt better than any smile could have.

Moments of silence ensued as Hannah came back from the kitchen and Dora and the cats came asking permission to climb over him again. With a nod of consent, he let them, sat back like a lion letting the kids of the pride have free range of his great body. Dora was now on her best behavior, imitating the cats in their sinuous grace as they showed him acceptance and affection with rubs and head butts. Andreas let them have their fill of exploring the body that was twice as big as the females they were used to, and must feel very different, too.

In the middle of playing, on cue at eight, Dora curled over his chest and promptly fell asleep.

Andreas sat there looking down at her as if he'd had a live grenade tossed in his lap.

Naomi rose to take her, and his whisper, dark and hushed, stopped her in her tracks. "She looks exactly like Petros."

Swallowing the immediate lump in her throat, Naomi nodded. "Yeah, only with Nadine's eyes."

He made no response, his gaze pinned on Dora's peaceful face as she surrendered to slumber in the security of his presence.

Long moments passed before he finally spoke. "If she's anything like him on the inside, she'll turn out to be an angel."

Her heart felt too full to make an answer, so Naomi merely reached for Dora. He made no move to help as she carried her away, nor offered to accompany her as she put her in bed.

Once Naomi came back, Andreas turned his gaze from Hannah to her. "You must be tired, too. Hannah said you wake up early with Dora, and that makes your days even longer."

"I don't know about Naomi, but that's definitely it for me." Hannah stood, stifling a yawn.

Andreas rose to his feet at once, making Naomi blink.

He'd never stood when she did, at least not out of gentlemanly politeness.

But she hadn't observed him around others much, certainly never with an older lady. Maybe it was his old-world Greek blood kicking in or something.

He shook Hannah's hand with what passed for warmth in his book, and again thanked her for her hospitality and for sharing her evening and kitchen with him.

Hannah fairly swooned with delight as she assured him the pleasure had definitely been hers. She met Naomi's eyes briefly as she rose to kiss her good-night. It was clear the woman thought Andreas was a god and that it would be Naomi's phenomenal luck if he was interested in her. It was clear Hannah would do anything to facilitate that interest. Such as pretending to be unable to keep her eyes open so Andreas would have time alone with Naomi, if only minutes before he left.

As soon as she'd disappeared, Naomi turned to Andreas.

Having him alone for the first time tonight, she couldn't wait anymore for all the things she was dying to know.

Why had he come? Why had he been this way all evening? What did he decide? And most important of all…what would he do now? Right this second?

He strolled past the coffee table, approaching her. "Thank you for this evening, Naomi."

She stood rooted, waiting for him to reach her.

He didn't. He headed in the other direction, and was halfway out of the room when she realized he was leaving.

Did he want her to run after him, ask him to stay? Was this to make up for when she'd told him to get out?

Though he'd better not get used to it, she had no choice but to bow to his wishes now. He'd yet to tell her what he'd decided.

Rushing after him, she caught up with him at the door.

He turned after he opened it, and it felt like a reversal of those last moments in his suite. His gaze was at its most unfathomable as he looked at her. Her blood surged to every inch of skin nearest to him, seeking his touch, begging his assuagement.

If he kissed her now, what would she do? Just let him, or meet him halfway?

He only said, "*Kalinychta*, Naomi," and walked out.

Unable to believe he'd just said good-night and left, she staggered forward, gripping the door for support. Her aching eyes clung to him as he walked away, willing him to turn so she could show him she wanted him to come back, to carry her to bed and end this gnawing hunger.

He just kept going, bypassed the elevator and headed for the stairwell. In seconds she heard his footfalls, sure and steady on the marble steps, receding until they were no more.

With her heart clanging in her chest, she shakily closed the door and leaned on it, disbelief expanding inside her.

He'd gone.

But…had he really gone, or would he come back?

If he didn't tonight, when would he?

Andreas didn't come back.

After a couple days of absence and silence, suspicion had started to gel in her mind. Then more days passed, and she could no longer find any other explanation.

That evening he'd spent with them must have been a test, to see if he could bear having them around. And he'd found he couldn't.

He might have also been trying to decide if he still wanted her, and had discovered that he didn't.

It seemed that night they'd shared, what had re-ignited her need for him, had only managed to purge her from his system. He'd had the closure sex she'd deprived him of when she'd walked away so abruptly. Now he had no more use for her. And he'd decided to leave her and Dora alone.

Mentally, she knew she should be feeling relieved, that Dora was safe. But she wasn't. She was only disappointed.

No, she wasn't disappointed.

She was crushed.

It felt as if she'd lost him all over again.

But it was even worse this time.

This time he'd shown her a glimpse of what she'd dreamed of from the moment she'd first seen him. A taste of Andreas the man, the companion, not only the lover and devourer.

And it had been ambrosia. She craved more of the closeness and fun and spontaneity that he'd given her during that magical evening.

And he'd just walked away. After he'd released

the slow poison of longing all over again in her blood. A more potent one this time, since he'd shown her that what she'd longed for wasn't a mirage. It could be real. It *was* real. But it would never be hers.

As he never would be.

Eight

"I was beginning to think you'd never come."

Naomi winced at Selene's brightness. She couldn't tell her she was late because she had been debating not coming. It had taken her all morning to summon the guts to bundle up Hannah and Dora and drive to Manhattan Beach.

Not that Andreas had factored in her dread of attending the Sarantos family gathering Selene and Aristedes had invited her to. It was a "family" gathering, and he was the man who had no relations with his.

She'd ended up coming because she wanted a relationship with them, for Dora's sake. Aristedes had said they'd all considered Petros a brother, and no matter how Naomi felt, she'd do anything to give Dora uncles and aunts who cared about her, and kids her age to grow up among.

Selene linked her arm through hers after she'd kissed and welcomed Hannah and Dora. "No more wasting time, ladies. Everybody is dying to meet you all."

Walking into the waterfront villa was like stepping through a wormhole and landing in Crete. The Greek influences in design were prevalent throughout, even if the traditional touches were imbued with the latest in modernity. It stood to reason that would be the Sarantoses' choice, since both Aristedes and Selene were of Greek origin.

It was sumptuous yet unpretentious, spacious yet not massive, a testament to the taste and priorities of those who'd built it. While the man of the house could afford something a hundred times more luxurious, he and his wife cared only about comfort, privacy, safety…and each other.

Naomi's observations ended when she found the Sarantos family coming to meet them en masse. What with the four sisters, their husbands and children, and a few more people who were close friends or distant relatives, she could barely keep up with the introductions and the new faces.

The only ones who stood out were Caliope, Andreas's youngest sibling, and her Russian husband, Maksim Volkov, one of the world's biggest steel magnates. With brothers like Aristedes and Andreas, Caliope could have fallen only for someone as overwhelming.

Suddenly, Naomi's heart rammed the base of her throat.

Strolling in from the terrace, framed by the breathtaking vista of the Atlantic, was Andreas.

Everyone's voices rose as he came to stand at the periphery of the gathering, ignoring everyone who scolded him for being late in welcoming Naomi and the others.

"Naomi, Hannah." That was the sum total of his acknowledgment of their presence before he turned his gaze down to Dora, who'd left her newfound friends and was crawling toward him at high speed.

He let her reach him, pull herself up his leg, and only when she gave him the most endearing grin in history did he relent and pick her up.

Voices rose again, some laughingly claiming it had to be the end of the world, others complaining that he hadn't given *their* kids that unprecedented privilege.

Andreas gave them all a serene look as Dora nuzzled his neck. "I didn't pick Dorothea up. She compelled me. Didn't you see that glance and grin? Ask Naomi. This child is an expert in getting whatever she sets her sights on, and she must have wanted to see what it's like being at this altitude. I don't volunteer pickup services, but when *your* kids lay claim to them like Dorothea did, I will comply."

Everyone laughed and ribbed him about turning out to be a huge rattle toy just like everyone else. But Naomi knew it wasn't true. If Dora had resorted to her demanding ways, he wouldn't have picked her up. But he'd had her trained from just their one encounter.

Andreas would never take the first step, or respond to approaches, until they were made to his strict specifications.

After making the connection with Andreas, Dora asked to be let down so she could rejoin the kids, who ranged in age from one to seven. Then everyone started drifting into smaller groups.

They all seemed to be leaving Naomi with Andreas on purpose. The moment they were alone, he said he was going back out on the terrace. She followed, only because she wanted to blast him apart.

He was braced with outstretched arms on the balustrade, his hair ruffling in the breeze, his gaze searching the horizon by the time she was at his side.

Snatching a glance back, to make sure they were out of earshot of the others, she fixed her eyes to the same point in the distance. "What are you doing here?"

"Right this second?" The voice that was as deep as that ocean, as alluring and merciless, washed over her. "I'm looking at the ocean."

She turned to him, found him regarding her in amusement, which he seemed to think she'd reciprocate.

She didn't find turmoil amusing. Nothing had explained the past ten days other than that he'd come, seen, conquered, then left. And just as she'd resigned herself that she would never see him again, she found him here. And could think of no good reason for that.

"How about a real answer?"

His lips twisted quizzically. "What's your theory about my presence? You must have come up with a few."

"Just one. You're toying with me."

He frowned. "How and why would I do that?"

The sudden seriousness in his eyes, that tinge of confusion, of dismay, deflated the bubbling accusations.

Had she gotten it all wrong, again? Could it be he'd just decided to visit his family and it had nothing to do with her?

The terrible thing was, that made sense. To go to the effort of toying with her, he'd have to think about her first. And he seemed to have dropped her from his consideration.

Without another word or look, she turned and walked back inside, wishing she could just take Hannah and Dora and leave.

God, why had she come? She should have never wished for more, even for Dora, just protected what they had. Now every exposure to his family—and him, now that he'd gotten it into his mind to start seeing them—would chip away at her. He'd already damaged her. More injuries might cripple her for good.

All her senses screamed a warning that Andreas was approaching. She lengthened her stride, reaching for the sanctuary of company.

Before he caught up with her, she fell into step with Caliope, who'd just left one of her older sisters.

Caliope turned with a radiant smile, stopping and forcing her to, as well. "Back already? Is it as nippy outside as it looks?" Her turquoise eyes went over Naomi's head. "Or is it another temperature-compromised reason that sent you back so soon?"

"All this creativeness to call me cold, Cali?" Andreas tutted.

"Not cold, my dearest brother, cool. Maddeningly so."

"Another lie, since I'm not your 'dearest' brother. We all know I'm at the end of the list of dearness around here."

Caliope laughed, not contradicting him, but clearly very fond of him. Andreas made people love him without doing a thing. Or while doing everything to make them hate him.

"It's just lack of exposure. Let us see you and you'd climb the list and share the top spots in no time."

"Hmm. That's all it takes? That might be arranged."

Caliope's eyes widened. "Really?" Without warning, she jumped forward and wrapped her arms around his neck. "Oh, yes, please, Andreas."

He looked as if he'd been hit by lightning.

This probably was the first time Caliope had hugged him.

Naomi could only hope he wouldn't rebuff her eagerness.

Then, as if approaching an abandoned package that might explode, he slowly wrapped his arms around his sister.

Yelping in delight, Caliope surged up to kiss him exuberantly.

Evidently thinking things had gone far enough, Andreas eased his hold on her and straightened to his full height.

No doubt knowing she'd gotten more than she could have expected, Caliope let him go with a sigh of contentment. "Man, I can't believe I have your promise we'll be seeing more of you. After you attended my wedding, too. Have I told you how much that meant to me?"

His lips twisted. "Only thirty-four times."

"Oh, I thought it was thirty-*five*."

"Four. It's how many times you've called me since."

Caliope's mouth dropped open. "You count people's calls?"

"Only yours…and Aristedes's. He always has

something earth-shattering to tell me, while you, *mikrá* Cali, I dread even more."

Caliope laughed again, turning to Naomi. "Do I look tiny to you? But that gives you an idea when the last time Andreas *really* saw me was." She turned back to her brother. "And what was so dreadful about my calls? I only updated you about where each of us was, to see if you could drop by."

"It's your efforts to 'remodel' me that I dread."

Caliope looked back at Naomi with a conspiring grin. "I think I can abandon all my efforts now, don't you think?"

Meaning that Naomi would be the one doing the remodeling? If only Caliope knew.

But she wasn't about to correct her assumptions. All she wanted was to escape this scene of familial reacquaintance, and Andreas, until she could leave. She would never come within a mile of any Sarantos ever again.

Andreas's eyes had turned to her, as if expecting her to respond to his sister, before being drawn back to Caliope when she winced and started stroking her belly.

He frowned. "You all right?"

"Oh, it's just Tatjana's daily acrobatic exercises."

His eyebrows rose. "You already named her?"

Caliope chuckled. "We decided on Tatjana Anastasia, after Maksim's mother and late sister, before we found out the sex. Then we did, and that was it."

Something like indulgence hovered over his lips. "I thought you looked your most beautiful at your wedding, but you've…blossomed since. Cliché, I know, but nothing else would do. Married life has been good to you. After a few bumps, that is."

"Maksim has been good to me. Phenomenal wouldn't even cut it. And those bumps only made things better."

Andreas whistled. "Better than phenomenal? Maksim must be some kind of supernatural being."

Caliope's grin was so bright, it nearly blinded Naomi. "He is."

"Glad to know I'm related through marriage to a superhero. He might come in handy."

Caliope poked him. "You should try them, you know."

"Maksim or bumps?"

Poking him harder with an unfettered laugh, Caliope flashed a devouring glance at her husband, who was watching her in the same way even as he talked to her sister Melina.

It was impossible to see those two together,

just like Selene and Aristedes, and not be buffeted by the force of emotions they shared. But there seemed something extra between Caliope and Maksim. According to Selene, they'd been through hell and back together, and it had clearly fused them in ways that the most sublime happiness couldn't have. Maksim looked at their child, Leo, and Caliope's advanced bump as if he were watching his own beating heart. As for how he looked at Caliope...it made Naomi's hair stand on end. It was almost too much love to witness.

Still chuckling, Caliope said, "Sorry, Maksim is taken, for this life and whatever comes next. You go get your own bumps with your own soul mate."

Naomi escaped Caliope's glance, which swerved to her, only to find her eyes colliding with Andreas's.

Slowly releasing her gaze, he turned to his sister. "Don't I require a soul first?"

"Oh, you have one somewhere. Even if it's buried under decades of dust. All we need to do is unearth it."

"As long as you leave the unearthing to me and don't try to precipitate it with your drilling methods."

After that, Caliope's direct comments forced

Naomi to participate in the conversation, until Hannah called her away, thankfully, to inform her that she was taking Dora to the pool.

Afterward, counting the seconds until she could leave, Naomi tried to respond to everyone's welcome and reciprocate their interest. It was as if all present considered her and her family theirs already. Which only made her decision not to see them anymore harder.

But one thing made it easier to forget her turmoil: the rich family spectacle unfolding before her eyes. Everyone weaved such a complex tapestry of relationships and emotions, it was fascinating to watch them interact. With her own father dying when she was five, only a year after Nadine was born, and growing up with just her mother, an only child, and Hannah for family, Naomi had never known what an extended one was like.

The most interesting part to her was when their reactions and interactions involved Andreas. It was clear they loved him, not that even they seemed to know why. And it was equally clear they didn't know what to make of him or of his unaccustomed presence among them today.

But her real fascination was in watching Andreas. Though there was nothing too overt, she started to believe that he actually cared about them, especially Aristedes and Caliope.

At one point, Naomi found herself with Caliope again. This time she told her the story of their early life in Crete, mainly about their parents' dysfunctional relationship.

Their father had been a charmer and a user who'd drifted in and out of their mother's life, each time coming back to add another child to his brood and take all she had, before disappearing again. He'd vanished from their lives for good when Caliope was not yet born, leaving their mother heartbroken and unwilling to go on.

This made Naomi look at Andreas in a new light.

Had he inherited his lack of emotion from their father? The others seemed unscathed by the man's genes. Aristedes seemed to have emotions in abundance, while Caliope had said her late brother, Leonidas, had been the most loving man on earth. So had Andreas been the only one who'd won the lottery of their father's terrible legacy?

From then on, Naomi watched him even more closely. Whenever she could find him. He disappeared for stretches of time before reappearing again at random.

She wondered if she had only imagined that he

cared for his family. Had she merely seen what she'd wanted to see, still hoping to find something redeemable about him?

But whatever he felt or didn't feel for them, it wasn't relevant where she was concerned. Though he did talk to her during the evening, it was in conversations involving others. Like that evening in her apartment, he made no effort to be alone with her. If she'd needed any reinforcement of her previous analysis, that gave it to her in spades.

He no longer wanted her.

While it hurt like she hadn't thought anything could ever again, at least it meant Dora was safe.

At the end of the evening, as everyone kissed her and she made promises that she knew she wouldn't keep, Andreas stood apart, watching her and his family. Just watching.

Hannah went ahead to put the sleeping Dora in her car seat before catching a ride to her daughter's house. While she did that occasionally on weekends, Naomi suspected she was doing it tonight hoping for something to develop in her absence. Turning away with a generalized good-night and thanks to everyone, Naomi rushed after her.

She wanted this over with...*now*.

She was almost outside the door when she

found Andreas beside her. "Did you enjoy your-self today?"

Feeling seconds away from tears, she nodded without raising her gaze to his.

"Dorothea and Hannah seemed to enjoy them-selves, too."

God, now she knew what a mouse felt like being tormented by a majestic, indifferent feline.

"Everyone loved having you all here."

She almost rounded on him and screamed, *"Everyone but you. And just what do you want now? It's sure not me."*

Out loud she said nothing, concentrating on counting the steps till she reached her car and es-cape.

He kept up with her until she got into it, kept the door open before she could slam it.

Bending, he seared her with his steady gaze. "I was coming to your place tomorrow, but I thought I'd give you a heads-up, since you're not big on surprises."

Fury at his presumption burned away her mis-ery. "Or on people deciding to drop by without consulting me."

"I am consulting you now."

"You're *informing* me, only so graciously ahead of time."

There was this confusion in his eyes again, as if he had no idea why she was so agitated. And why would he?

"May I come over tomorrow, Naomi?"

So we can start this maddening merry-go-round again?

Out loud she only managed a terse, "No."

Then she pulled the door from his hand. He stood there as she turned the car on and drove away slowly.

She arrived at home an hour later, put Dora in bed and did all her nightly rituals. Then she slipped between the covers…and finally let the tears fall.

Nine

Naomi woke up to find her pillow soaked.

The first thing she did was punch it.

As she should have Andreas. Long ago.

And when the opportunity presented itself, what had she done? A few chest thumps and a couple slaps. The huge lout must still be laughing his head off.

Jumping from bed, determined to leave him and any thoughts of him behind, she rushed about her morning routine before Dora woke up. Though judging from the sounds of deep breathing over the baby intercom, she was too soundly asleep to wake up soon. Playing nonstop with so many kids yesterday had wiped her out.

Naomi had just finished making coffee when the bell rang. Thinking it must be the super, she rushed to the door.

She took a look through the peephole…and lurched back.

Andreas.

She took another look. Because it wasn't *only* Andreas.

Another Peek confirmed the absurdity of the first one.

It was him. And flowers.

Andreas? Bringing her *flowers*?

And not just any flowers. A bouquet half her size, with every type of gold blossom, with the stems and leaves tinted turquoise.

Her head spun. Was he exhibiting his father's condition? He'd return, then leave, then return and so on, in an endless loop, until he wrecked her?

She didn't think so. She might have been a victim of her craving for him so far, but no longer.

She spoke loudly enough for him to hear her through the thick door. "Go away, Andreas."

His answer was immediate. "No, I won't."

"Then you'll stand there until you have to leave."

"I'll stand here until *you* have to leave."

"I'm not leaving for the whole weekend."

"Then that is how long I'll stand here."

And the worst thing? She believed he would.

"I still won't talk to you when you finally ambush me."

"You're talking to me now. Might as well make it about something constructive."

"Here's something constructive. I'm allergic to flowers."

"No, you're not."

"I'm allergic to *you*."

He gave a long-suffering exhalation. "Apparently I do elicit inexplicable reactions in you."

"Oh, those reactions are very explicable."

"Not to me. Enlighten me."

"Listen, this is just silly."

"First thing we agree on today."

It was her turn to sigh. "Did Aristedes put you up to this? Or was it Selene or Caliope who advised the flowers? It was probably a committee decision, especially with this over-the-top bouquet that mirrors my coloring."

"I can understand your skepticism. But no, the flowers and their color connotations are my own initiative. I bet the others wouldn't have suggested something you found so aggravating. But as ridiculous as it sounds now, I thought flowers would provide an opening in the impasse we inexplicably reached last night, or a peace offering in this one-sided war you've resumed for no discernible reason."

"You're that lost in your own world? You see no reason?"

"None."

"How about that I'm not at your disposal to disappear and then return, pretending nothing happened?"

"I didn't disappear."

"What do you call what you did for the three days after you met Aristedes?"

"After you had Aristedes issue me a cease and desist, you mean. And I call it 'giving you time to calm down.'"

"Calm down? When I was going out of my mind needing to know what the meeting achieved, what you decided?"

"I thought you wouldn't want to hear from me directly, and that Aristedes would tell you how things went."

"How could he? He didn't know what you'd decided, either, which left me even more agitated until I heard from you. Then you came, spent the whole evening with us and didn't say a word. After which you disappeared again for a week. And the next time I saw you it was by accident. And you still said nothing!"

"It wasn't by accident."

That stopped her ready volley. Then she huffed a harsh laugh. "And to think I believed you weren't toying with me."

"Why would you think I was? When did I ever 'toy' with you?"

"That's the euphemism I came up with for the manipulation you've been exposing me to since you came back."

"How was it manipulation, when I said I would claim Dorothea, not take her from you?"

He had said "claim" not "take." But the rest…

Suddenly everything inside her was like one of Hannah's knitting balls after Loki and Thor had had their way with it.

"As for the second instance of disappearance you claim, it took me that long to put together that family event."

She snatched the door open. "What?"

Everything seemed to spin around her as the sight of him impacted her senses. He stood there, legs braced apart, as if preparing for a grueling fight, the gigantic bouquet gripped in one hand beside a long, powerful thigh. He looked a few light-years beyond fantastic. Though on closer inspection he had a haggard look about him. And was that the same suit he'd had on last night?

"Can I come in now?"

"Did you just say this so you can come in?"

"I have plenty of vices, Naomi. Lying isn't one of them."

He was right. And since he never lied, in light of all he'd said, had she jumped to conclusions about everything?

Oh, she didn't know anything anymore.

Exasperated, with herself more than anything, she stepped aside with an ill-tempered huff.

His raised eyebrow as he brushed past her made her bristle more. "No comments about my lack of graciousness?"

"I wouldn't dream of it. I now know how sharp your claws are, and I need my eyes where they are."

He headed to the family room, put down the bouquet, then turned to her with an expression that looked like disappointment, then morphed at once into anxiety. "Why isn't Dorothea up yet?"

Wondering if she'd read him right, Naomi said, "She's just sleeping off yesterday's unusual exertion."

He seemed unconvinced. "Hannah said she wakes up no later than six. It's nine. And she spent a lot of time in the sun and the pool. Maybe too much. Maybe she's not well."

"How do you know that?"

"I was with her most of that time."

So that was where he'd kept disappearing yesterday.

Then anxiety burst inside her as his words sank in. She'd left Dora to Hannah's care, never doubting that she'd know what was enough. But… Had Dora's breathing been too deep? Could she be suffering from sunstroke? She could be burning up….

Naomi bolted to her room, feeling Andreas hot on her heels. Braking at the door, she opened it with all the control she had left, turning to Andreas to signal *quiet*. He nodded, followed her soundlessly to Dora's crib.

Naomi's heart hammered as she bent to press her cheek to her forehead…and all tension deflated. It was cooler than her own hectic flesh.

Before she could turn to Andreas, he bent, spooning her. Her breath caught even as she realized he was just unable to wait to find out if Dora was okay, was reaching out to check her temperature, too.

As soon as his large palm cupped the baby's cheek, she gurgled something contented and caught his hand and swept it with her as she turned noisily to her side.

They ended up standing there, with him bent over her, both trapped with his hand held beneath Dora's cheek.

"Will she wake up if I withdraw my hand?" His whisper tickled Naomi's ear, poured right into her brain.

Turning her head, she found her lips in his neck, and somehow managed to whisper back, "She's bound to wake up soon, anyway."

"I'd rather it's not me who woke her up."

"It's actually better if you do. Oversleeping will throw her whole pattern out of whack."

"In that case, go ahead and wake her."

"Withdraw your hand first and let's see if that does it."

He tried, but Dora only whimpered and clung to it.

"So much for that. Let's go for a more direct approach," Naomi murmured. His other hand came around her, stopping hers as she reached for Dora, enveloping her whole body in his.

Everything inside her fell apart as she turned

to him and found him gazing at Dora, his face gripped in some fierce…emotion?

"She looks so content sleeping."

His whisper was the deepest Naomi had ever heard, almost reverent. There was no doubt anymore what this was about.

He didn't have the heart to wake Dora up.

Andreas now had a heart?

From all signs so far with the baby, it seemed he was sprouting one where there'd been none before.

Shaken by the idea, Naomi let her voice get louder, since she'd decided Dora should wake up. "You won't remember those moments when she's cranky and whining later because she's tired and can't fall asleep…because you let her oversleep."

He grimaced, gave an apology in Greek then withdrew his hand from Dora's grip, firmly but still gently. There *was* gentleness this time, not only the clinical care he'd demonstrated before.

Dora protested and turned on her back, her eyes fluttering open. Naomi heard Andreas catch his breath.

Shutting out the disturbing observations, she stroked Dora's head. "Enough charging, darling. It's time to wake up."

As always, Dora woke up with no disorientation.

Her eyes crinkled in pleasure at seeing Naomi, before bypassing her and rounding with surprise at finding Andreas there.

Naomi felt man and baby lock gazes, and held her breath. Then Dora squealed in excitement, rolled to her side and climbed up the rails of her crib. Once propped up, she bobbed up and down, eyes luminous with glee, her grin showing every tooth she'd sprouted.

Andreas reached out a tentative hand to stroke Dora's cheek. "Does she always wake up excited like this?"

Naomi's throat tightened. "She is sunny most of the time, and wakes up in a great mood. But this is extra."

"She must be too used to you to make such a fuss every morning. I must be a novelty."

Acute honesty forced Naomi to correct his assumption. "She never greets new people with this fanfare."

His eyes widened. "Really?"

"Really. We got her a wonderful stand-in nanny, and she vetoed her. Our neighbors, a really nice couple, had dinner with us a few weeks ago and she ignored them completely."

Andreas looked so pleased, Naomi almost had to

rub her eyes. But there was no doubt about it. He was thrilled Dora was treating him preferentially.

What the hell. Let him have more proof of his supreme influence on any being that breathed.

Naomi sighed. "Are you waiting for her to ask to be picked up in the exact way you trained her to?"

Andreas blinked. "That was when she was being bratty. Now she's being…"

"Delightful?" Naomi suggested when he couldn't find the right word, and he nodded. "So what are you waiting for? All these squats mean she can't wait for you to pick her up."

He reached down for Dora, his large palms spanning her rib cage as she kicked and gurgled in delight. "*Sygnómi*, Dorothea. Climbing my leg was much more understandable."

Hearing him apologizing so earnestly to Dora had a weird effect on Naomi. She burst out laughing.

Both man and baby turned to her in astonishment.

"Don't mind me. Carry on," she spluttered as she headed to the changing table. Andreas followed her when she beckoned, relinquishing Dora to her with utmost reluctance. He stood watching intently, showing no signs of distaste, as she changed the baby.

Then she stood aside and let him pick her up again. When he apologized for not being the one to change her, as he had to learn first, Naomi laughed again and headed out to the kitchen.

Andreas followed, Dora in his arms, cats around his legs, that famous eyebrow raised.

Naomi didn't press the issue of his reason for being here as she got things out for breakfast, while he put Dora in her high chair as if this was his morning routine, and Dora asked adorably for her toys.

He joined Naomi in preparing breakfast, admitting that he'd had none. As they worked in tandem, there was again a pervasive ease and companionship. This time she was certain it wasn't something he did on purpose. It was simply…there.

As if by agreement, they didn't bring up anything during breakfast.

Afterward, once in the family room, after she'd distributed his bouquet into four vases, with Dora and the cats busy together, he explained that tidbit that had made her open the door.

"After I left that evening, I knew I needed to get

my family together to meet you and Dora. I had to get a place first."

"What? You mean that house in Manhattan Beach wasn't Aristedes's and Selene's?"

"No. Their home is a couple miles away, though."

That stunned her. Though…thinking back, she recalled they'd invited her to a "family gathering," not to "our place," and no one had implied the home was theirs. Had they all been in it together, leaving it vague, so she wouldn't realize? But why?

"It took a week to finalize the deal, get the place ready to receive people and to gather everyone."

He'd gone to all this expense and effort to put that day together? Which would have been wonderful for her, had she known all that, but…

"You went to these lengths, just to end up ignoring me?"

His eyes widened. "Where do you keep getting those interpretations for my actions? I was giving you a chance to get to know the zillion members of my family. I thought we could talk some other time. Not that you seemed to want to see me at all. Though I now realize why."

So she'd gotten that wrong, too.

"You could have told me any of that," she mumbled.

"You mean alert you to my plans beforehand, so you'd surprise me by not attending? Didn't even occur to me."

"You could have called."

He shook his head. "To say what? I was still taking the steps to try to reach the decision you wanted to hear."

It was her turn to shake her head. He had no clue, did he? But he had gone to all this trouble for Dora. It proved he'd had powerful feelings for Petros, even if Naomi hadn't understood the connection or seen its evidence. Now, from the times he'd seen Dora, that first reconnaissance evening, his vigilant day yesterday, and this morning, it was clear he'd already developed an attachment to her, and she to him.

So had his emotions been dormant, and it had taken what he'd viciously said he'd never have—a child—to awaken them?

This made sense. Perfect sense. It also explained why he hadn't tried to touch Naomi in over ten days.

This was no longer about her in any way.

"I never told you about me and Petros."

His solemn tone brought her focus back to him. "You never told me anything, Andreas."

He nodded. Acknowledging, making no excuses.

But from the way his steely eyes smoldered, it seemed he'd tell her something now. Something seriously important.

"Before I do, you have to know about my family. My father was a useless, selfish son of a bitch we scarcely saw, and my mother was a silly, sentimental pushover he used up, with us scrambling in the middle. Aristedes, being the oldest, was the one who bore the main brunt of it all, dropping out of school to work four jobs to support us when he was only thirteen."

Wanting to spare him retelling this part, Naomi interrupted. "Caliope told me all that yesterday."

He exhaled. "But what she couldn't tell you, since neither she nor anyone else knows it, is that by the time I was that age, as the 'man of the house' in my elders' absence, I had to fend for my family of women and babies in different ways. There was this gang who 'ruled' the area, and the only way any household could be safe from them was if they 'volunteered' a son to their service. I volunteered myself, for my family and Petros's."

Naomi sat forward, her heart racing. She'd never expected anything like that. Which was naive, to think such poverty hadn't exposed him to crime and criminals.

But his had been more than simple exposure. "You volunteered yourself in Petros's place?"

"There was no choice, really. He'd always been the gentle soul you knew. He wouldn't have survived a day as a gang member, while I was already almost six feet tall, and I oozed aggression and fearlessness. The gang leader took a shine to me, trained me himself, then put me to work."

The way he'd said that. Work. She saw a world of pain and ugliness and fear in it, of danger and damage and degradation.

She couldn't ask for specifics. Whatever he'd done, he'd been a minor and he'd been coerced, with his family and Petros's held as hostages.

"Then, three years later, Aristedes took us to the States. I kept it a secret or they wouldn't have let me go—or worse. But I promised Petros I'd take care of him. I worked while studying, and sent him all the money I made to support his sick parents and pay the protection money the gang demanded in lieu of my services. But when I went back for him as soon as I finished college, I found them in abject poverty. The gang had been taking every dollar I sent. Then they asked for three million dollars to let me take Petros and his parents with me. They wanted me to ask Aristedes for the money, but I refused to drag him into this. So they gave me another option. To be 'theirs' for five years. I agreed."

Naomi's heart squeezed until she felt it would rupture.

He'd entered into indentured slavery for his friend!

"And for the next five years, they put my 'talents' to use, defrauding and embezzling countless millions for them."

God. If hearing about this oppressed and enraged her that much, how had it felt living through it?

"But as the fifth year drew to an end, it became clear I was too lucrative for them to ever let me go. So I confronted the boss, my original recruiter and 'mentor.' It enraged him that after all he'd done for me, I wanted to leave him."

"He destroyed your life!" she cried out. "He *enslaved* you! Was he insane as well as a monster?"

"He wasn't exactly sane in the way he viewed me. He considered me his firstborn, as none of his sons had followed in his footsteps, and he'd bestowed his 'fatherly' pride on me. From my uncomplaining efficiency, he'd thought I'd become fully engaged in his way of life, and he'd planned to surprise me at the end of that five-year test of his. Instead of cutting me loose, he would have made me his heir, bypassing his own sons. I had one father who didn't know I was alive, and when I stumbled on another, he became obsessed with me."

"And he thought you should love him for it and be grateful, huh? I can't even imagine how you felt, but just hearing about it makes me so mad I could kill that man."

"Don't bother. I already did."

Her jaw dropped. "Y-you…?"

"I killed him. In self-defense…I guess."

Beyond shocked, she could barely articulate the question. "W-what do you mean?"

"He said I was destroying all his hopes, but I wasn't walking away with all his secrets. In one of the rare times I ever got angry, I told him what I thought of him, I guess breaking whatever he had for a heart that morbidly loved me. Bad mistake, since he came after me with his favorite machete. Then he was lying at my feet…dead."

"So why do you say you 'guess' it was self-defense? It was!"

"I say so because he was much older and I had

long surpassed him in expertise with weapons. It was crystal clear to me during that explosive fight that it was him or me. But I don't know if I thought that because I was in danger in those moments, or because I knew that if I only stopped him then, he would still have me killed eventually. Then what was to become of Petros and his folks? To this day I don't know what is true."

"Then it was self-defense and in defense of others, too."

His eyes thanked her for her fierceness, but didn't concede that verdict. "Whatever it was, I got away with it. I turned myself in, but the Cretan police were so thrilled someone had finally rid them of that kingpin, and seemed extra glad that it was me who'd done it. Seemed they knew exactly what he'd done to me. Their official report said it was a hired assassin from a rival gang, and they even helped me take Petros and his family out of Crete. I'd just gotten them settled here, thinking I had finally escaped this nightmare, when I discovered that it wasn't over, not by a long shot."

When he paused, Naomi grabbed his forearm. "Just say everything at once!"

He looked surprised at her agitation, but pleased by the evidence of her involvement in his story.

Then his gaze looked into the past again. "The man's wife, who became the new kingpin in her husband's place, called me. She somehow knew it was me who'd killed her husband. And she pledged that as I'd deprived her of the love of her life, she would strike at my loved ones. I scoffed at her threat, told her I didn't have any, thanks to her late husband. I lost all contact with my family during the years of servitude to him. As for Petros, he wasn't a loved one but more of a…pet."

Naomi knew he'd had to say this to make that bitch lay off. It must have galled him having to do so. "Did she buy it?"

"I guess, about Petros. But she said that one day I would resume relationships with my family or make a new one. And that's when she'd strike."

All the missing shards hurtled together so fast, so hard in her mind, Naomi collapsed back on the couch under the barrage.

This…this was monstrous. And explained so much.…

"I knew she was capable of keeping me under surveillance forever, having laid their networks and provided their financing myself. But I didn't think it was such a big problem. I doubted my family wanted me back. But as the years passed, they tried to reconnect with me and I started feeling that ax hanging over my head more every day. Then I met you."

Every wisp of air left her in a rush.

"I suddenly couldn't let this go on anymore. So I went to Crete to negotiate an alliance with a rival cartel, to help me neutralize the threat from I Kyría, as she'd come to be known."

"W-was that the time you saved me and Malcolm from Christos Stephanides's thugs?"

"Yes. I knew Malcolm was courting my favor by planning to do business in my homeland. When I found out you were going with him, it brought things to a head and I decided it was time to seek that alliance."

"Were you following us that day?"

"I was following *you*."

So Nadine had been right.

He went on. "I know you think I saved you, but I don't believe Christos would have seen his threat through. He's not that bad. Nothing like the people I was mixed up with. That's why I succeeded in negotiating with him on your behalf, but failed in my own negotiations, since I couldn't offer my prospective allies full disclosure about why I needed their help."

"And money didn't work?"

"It doesn't work that way in these areas. It's people throwing their lots together and depending on each other to have each other's back, and it was a price I couldn't pay. I was never again becoming vulnerable to anyone."

"What happened then?" She could barely choke out the question.

"I did the stupidest thing I'd ever done in my life. I went back to the States and straight to Malcolm's office. I had an excuse to see you and I took it. And you approached me…and you know how that went. You were the first one I ever *wanted*, but I knew this was what I Kyría was waiting for. I knew you'd be her target if anyone ever found out about us."

So that was it. Why he'd so obsessively kept their relationship, then their marriage a total secret.

Only one question was left. "Why didn't you tell me?"

He huffed. "That I was a criminal and a murderer, and associating with me might make you target to a vengeful mob boss?"

Naomi found herself on her feet. "You're no such things! You were forced into whatever crimes you perpetrated. As for her, I would have understood the need for secrecy."

He seemed stunned by her reaction. "I didn't think you'd understand. I thought you'd just run away." He barked a harsh, ugly laugh. "But in the end, you ran because I *didn't* tell you, it seems. But I had hopes I could end this, and this was why I stalled you in that divorce. I'd been going all out to negotiate with I Kyría and she'd suddenly seemed amenable, had me doing things for her to 'atone.' Then after six months, she told me that she'd been only stringing me along, giving me hope before taking it away, and that I'd have to live like her forever, without having anyone close. Because the moment I came near to someone, anyone, she'd deprive me of them. She'd moved from bereaved to deranged, and her hatred of me had become what fueled her existence. I knew then that I'd gotten away with the time we had together, but we'd entered a whole new level, and no amount of secrecy or precautions would prove enough from then on. I signed the divorce papers then and just cut myself off from everyone, including Petros."

And everything finally made sense. Horrific sense.

"I couldn't come back even for Leonidas's funeral or Aristedes's wedding. I only went to Caliope's wedding because it was in the depths of Russia and a spur-of-the-moment affair that no one could have known about. But Petros and Nadine's funeral was announced, and you were there. I couldn't risk alerting her to your and Dorothea's existence."

This was atrocious. He'd been living in fear that he'd act as a bull's eye to whomever he was close to.

"Then how did you end up coming back?" she whispered.

"How do you think?"

"Y-you…?"

At her choking horror, his lips twisted. "Don't you think she deserved it?"

"Actually, yes, but…"

He ended her stammering. "Much as I had long wished to send her to her husband's side, I'm no killer. She just died. Thankfully. Not that I thought this would change anything. I was sure she left instructions to hound me into the next life. But I went to her funeral, anyway. No matter that she'd turned my life into hell, I did kill her husband and it was what sent her off the deep end. I wanted to make my peace with her."

Naomi exploded to her feet. "And what? Has she risen up from her grave and is after you as a zombie now?"

He tugged her back to the couch. "You managed all that, and now you flake out on me?"

"Dammit, Andreas," she shouted. "What happened?"

He exhaled. "Her oldest son approached me, said that whatever vendetta existed between me and his mother had died with her. He condemned his parents' criminal activities, and what they'd done to me. The man said he bore me no ill will, even begged my pardon."

"That was it? For real?"

"I know what you mean. I could hardly believe it myself. That no one was in danger because of me anymore. That I was free. For the first time since I was thirteen."

Naomi didn't know how she held back from throwing herself at him. Probably because she was paralyzed with so many realizations and emotions.

"I came back that same day. With the time difference, I arrived here to wait for you to come home."

Suddenly, she felt her consciousness begin to flicker.

He was...was...*smiling*.

Sinking back on the couch, she moaned, "What a time for you to crack your first real smile."

His grin widened even more. "It's just…phew, what a load off. I never told anyone any of this. Only Petros knew. And not everything. I never told him about my suspicion that I didn't kill that man in pure self-defense."

But you haven't told me *everything.* So many questions still clamored inside her.

Before she could ask any, he continued. "But I can't blame everything I am on these events. Even without this hanging over my head, I wasn't relationship material, not with my background."

"Your father, you mean?"

"And myself. With the kind of life I led, I never felt much for anyone."

She gaped at him. He really thought so.

She surged toward him, needing to put him straight. "You felt far more than most people ever could. You sacrificed yourself for your family's and Petros's safety."

He frowned at her. "I never looked at it that way, or that I did anything because of feelings. I thought I was responsible as the one who could do something about it all. So I did it."

"And to do it, you wouldn't let yourself feel, so

you'd operate on maximum efficiency unclouded by emotion."

He mulled over her statement, which he seemed to have never considered. "You might be right. I didn't let anything surface, not even anger. I got so used to being this way, I no longer knew if I had emotions lurking beneath or not. But then I was free of the threat that has defined my life, and free to honor Petros's will." Andreas suddenly took her hands in his. "And that was before I saw Dorothea. But now that I have, I want to far more than I ever thought I could. You might think it too soon for me to be saying this, and I know I'd never be the father Petros would have been, but I'll do my damnedest to be there for Dorothea in every possible way."

His impassioned pledge lodged right into Naomi's heart.

For she now knew without a doubt he meant it. And he would fulfill it. The Andreas who'd borne all that for the father would do even more for the daughter.

Holding back tears with difficulty, Naomi nodded. "You'd succeed in anything you put your mind to, Andreas."

"But I can only if I'm part of her daily life."

What about being part of *hers*, too?

But he'd just admitted she wasn't why he'd come back. She'd been incidental to his main objective.

An hour ago, *Naomi's* main objective had been to defend Dora and herself. But now, with their history rewritten, all she wanted was to give Andreas whatever he needed, to try to erase the pain and injustice he'd suffered, even at the expense of her own needs. There was only one answer she could give him.

"I'll agree to anything you want."

His eyes flared with relief, his hands squeezing hers in supplication. "Then move in with me."

Ten

"Move over, world, here comes super Dorothea!"

Naomi's eyes jerked up, the newspaper she'd been reading already forgotten.

But then this sight regularly made her forget the whole world. The sight of Andreas with Dora.

In workout pants and a tank top that showed off the poetry of his physique, Andreas was holding Dora up high in one hand. Clad in a bright red-and-blue jumpsuit, Dora was shrieking in delight as she held herself in a tight upward bow and spread out her arms and legs like a flying superhero.

It was his turn today to handle Dora's morning routine. She was one happy baby in general, but she reserved that extra edge of glee for her daddy.

And there was no doubt anymore *that* was what Andreas was becoming, or had already become, in the month since they'd moved with him into the house in Manhattan Beach.

A month when he'd been performing all possible fatherly chores for Dora, been the perfect host and housemate to them all and a great companion and friend to Naomi…and nothing more.

Not one single look or touch more.

Andreas approached the chuckling Hannah, swept Dora down for a smacking kiss, then did the same with Naomi, to Dora's raucous delight. He ended the aerial show by flipping her into her high chair, and when she yelled for more, he only raised an eyebrow and she at once changed her tone, pretended to clap, asking for her toys with utmost courteousness.

After he prepared her breakfast and poured himself a cup of coffee, Andreas came to sit across from Naomi at the huge kitchen island. "Doing anything special today?"

Hannah was the one who answered him. "I'm heading for Connecticut as soon as one of you comes home from work."

Andreas turned to Hannah. "You can go now so you can have the whole day with Susan. I'll do all my meetings online. Call Steve the moment you're ready to go."

Hannah, who never stopped being awed by Andreas's pampering, smiled with grateful pleasure. "That would be great to get a head start, even if I'm staying with Susan and the kids till the weekend. And I'll take Spiros if he's available. He's so entertaining to drive with."

Andreas gave her one of those smiles that progressively came easier to him. "Spiros it is." Then he turned to Naomi. "It's you and me, then. If you don't have something else planned, that is."

She was only glad she had. "Actually, I'm going out with Malcolm after work. We're meeting a couple of potential clients for dinner. What was this all about?'

His gaze betrayed nothing but mild if good-natured disappointment as he turned around to Dora. "Seems we'll celebrate alone, *mikri prinkipissa mou.*"

Naomi's heart trembled at the way he called Dora my little princess. "Celebrate what?"

"A milestone. You've all been here a month today."

"If only you'd given us a heads-up," Hannah lamented.

Andreas waved a hand. "There'll be other milestones." He rose to clean the mess Dora had made while attempting to eat alone, then started feeding her another portion to make up for what had ended up on the tray and floor. "Like Dorothea's first birthday in a month. We'll do something big then. How about that?"

After the two women approved of his plan, Hannah excused herself, giving Naomi a look that clearly meant: *Are you mad? Going out with Malcolm when you could be celebrating with Andreas? When I've left you two alone, too?*

Naomi escaped her gaze, pretended she had to run, kissed Dora and said a few vague things to Andreas before striding out.

She had to settle this with Hannah soon, so she'd stop trying to give her time alone with Andreas. To him, Naomi was now merely Dora's mother or caretaker…or whatever she was.

The irony never ceased to torment her. Now that he was free to feel, he couldn't feel even passion for her anymore.

But she knew this situation was the only logical solution. Even if it meant she would now have him constantly in her life…yet never have him at all.

All she could wish for was that one day, she'd be free of her feelings for him, too.

"I think this contract is ours, Naomi."

She smiled at Malcolm across the table. "We did give a damn irresistible pitch."

"We make an unstoppable team." Malcolm's eyes twinkled at her with their usual geniality, before an edge of seriousness entered them. "And I think it's a great time for us to take our teamwork and friendship further."

Oh, no. Please, God, *no…*

Malcolm went on, oblivious to her dismay. "Think how much more we can be for each other, Naomi. We'd make as great a team at home and as parents for Dora as we are at work."

She reached for his hand, squeezed it in a silent plea for him to stop. "If there was any chance I thought this would work, I would have made the first move, Malcolm. You would make the perfect husband for some incredibly lucky woman, like you once did for Zoe. But it won't be me. I love you, but I'll never be in love with you. And oh, God…I so hope this won't be a problem between us."

His expression reminded her of Andreas's earlier

today. Disappointed but understanding, and not a little self-deprecating. Then he covered the hand gripping his. "How can it be a problem? We're friends, with or without anything more developing. And that's the difference between us, I guess. I am not in love with you, either, but I don't think I'll ever be in love again, not after Zoe. I thought my feelings for you might be enough. But you're probably right and they aren't." Suddenly his smile widened. "Hey, did you know we might have a far bigger thing happening than this contract?"

Relieved he'd let it go this easily, and apparently with no hard feelings, she said, "What could be bigger than that?"

"Andreas Sarantos. He called yesterday and said he'd come in tomorrow to 'settle things.' I don't want to be overly optimistic, but I really think he'll finally put his financing magic behind SUN Developments"

Andreas hadn't told her about this. Just as she hadn't told Malcolm about what had been going on with him. But with Andreas no longer keeping their living arrangements a secret, she hated for her partner to find out from someone else.

So she told him everything. At least the part

about Petros's will and Dora, and their moving in with Andreas.

Malcolm listened in total astonishment, then finally whistled. "That's quite a radical change. How are you handling this?"

"It's been smooth," she lied. "Andreas makes everything so once he puts his mind to it."

"And you say Dora's taken to him."

"Dora adores him."

Malcolm's gaze became considering. "Is he the reason you didn't even consider my suggestion?"

"It's not because of him, no."

"Meaning he didn't make a move, but that doesn't stop you from being unable to consider anyone else, huh?"

Finding no more reason to deny this, at least to Malcolm, who was being so understanding, she nodded.

He leaned forward, his expression serious. "This has been going on with you all along, hasn't it? From way back when we first met Andreas?" She again nodded. "And him? I can't believe he hasn't snapped you up, especially now."

"I hate to use the cliché...but it's complicated."

Malcolm sighed. "I just bet it is."

After a moment of silence, she said, "Is it okay if we get going?"

Not that she wanted to return to where Andreas and his killer friendliness awaited her, but this confrontation, as wonderful as Malcolm was being, had left her drained.

"Sure."

After settling the bill, Malcolm courteously led her out of the restaurant.

As they waited for the valet to bring her car over, he turned to her with a frown. "You know, I'm no longer sure I want Andreas to take us on."

That stunned her. She grasped her partner's arm. "You're not letting what I told you influence you, are you? My personal situation has nothing to do with doing business with him."

"I actually think they're closely related. It all ties in to my faith in his judgment. An hour ago he was the guy who mines gold out of dross. Now he's the dolt who can't see the rare gem he literally has under his nose."

Her heart suddenly lifting at her friend's morale boost, she laughed. "Thank you, Malcolm."

"Maybe I'll keep our appointment only to find out what's wrong with him, and give him a piece of my mind."

"Oh, no, please don't even mention me. And don't you dare think of passing up this opportunity." She held his eyes until he nodded. "And, Malcolm…I'm sorry again if I disappointed you."

He waved her apology away. "You never disappoint me."

Overwhelmed by warmth for this man, she reached out to hug him. Malcolm hugged her back, before taking her arm with a grin and walking her to her car.

After closing her door, he leaned in the open window. "And, Naomi, relax, okay? We're good."

She nodded, profoundly grateful to have such a friend.

Then, waving to him with a broad smile, she drove away, her heart lighter than it had been in years.

By the time she entered Andreas's house, her heart was leaden again. It felt like going back to a prison cell every time she returned here.

She debated again if she should do something about it. Such as tell him how she felt. That she wanted him, and that if he still had any desire for her they should be together, and it wouldn't complicate being parents to Dora.

What always stopped her was her fear that she'd risk Dora's peace. For what would happen when Andreas had enough of her? Or wanted to replace her in his bed? Could she be certain that it wouldn't impact Dora?

Loki and Thor came rushing to welcome her, their presence, as always, a distraction from heart-aches.

Carrying them both, she kissed and cooed to them as she walked to the family room, expecting to find Andreas working on his laptop. She braced herself for his now usual pleasantness.

Her smile faltered when she found him standing in the middle of the room, barefoot, his shirt pulled out of his pants and open, an empty shot glass carelessly in hand.

His body seemed relaxed, but it was the way his head was tilted, the way he watched her from beneath lowered eyebrows, and the total absence of his now accustomed smile that made her feel like a deer walking into a mountain lion's ambush.

Her steps faltered as she approached him, bringing his face into focus. Its stark lines seemed to be hewn from granite, and his eyes crackled like lightning.

"Anything wrong? Is Dora all right?" she whispered, even though she instinctively knew this wasn't about Dora.

Without relinquishing her gaze, he bent and placed the glass on the coffee table. "Put the cats down, Naomi."

It was only then she noticed she was hugging them tightly, as if to hide behind them, and they were squirming to get away. Cursing silently, she released them, and they jumped down and ran off to indignantly groom themselves.

She raised uncertain eyes to Andreas as he approached her, deepening her feeling of being stalked. Her hand rose to her throat, where she felt her heart had migrated, and his gaze singed it before moving to her lips, then her eyes, sending her heartbeat into a crazy spiral.

His voice was a predator's growl. "For forty-one nights I've held back, Naomi, kept my distance, given you something different. Now, no more."

He'd counted the nights since they'd last made love? "Andreas..."

All thought evaporated as his arm shot out. Next second she was slamming against his unyielding power. Then the world spun upside down as he... he...

Andreas had hauled her over his shoulder!

Her lungs emptied on a cry of shock, every nerve firing as his fingers sank into her buttocks and thighs. Her senses churned as he strode down the hallway, her world turning into a swirl of vertigo and overstimulation.

Then he was sweeping her from his shoulder and tumbling her onto a bed. His bed. Where she hadn't been sleeping every night of the last hellish month.

Before her heart could spill the next batch of chaotic beats, he was straddling her and pushing her jacket off, then pulling her blouse along with her bra over her head. He slid off her, only to sweep her skirt and panties down her trembling legs.

"Andreas…" That was all she could say. She said it over and over like an invocation.

"*Ne.* Moan my name like that, Naomi, whimper it, and when I'm riding you, scream it."

She would have screamed it right then if she had breath left in her. But all she could do was lie there, enervated, watching him push away and up to rid himself of his clothes with the same barely contained ferocity and haste. Then he fell back on top of her, like a starving predator over his willing prey.

He squashed her shuddering breasts beneath the

hardness of his hair-roughed chest, rubbed against her until she keened and writhed to intensify the contact.

"This…this is what I've gone stark-raving insane for all those forty-one nights, Naomi. *This.*"

He bore down on her, grinding his huge, marble-smooth and hard erection into her mound. Her thighs fell wide apart and her back arched, begging for his total invasion.

He dragged her head back with a hand bunched in her hair as his lips latched on to hers. His roughly devouring kisses trailed down her cheeks, jaw and neck, drawing on her flesh, wrenching out every spark of desire from every blood cell, until she felt her very life force rushing into him. She tried to draw in a breath, but he lifted her off the bed, twisted her around and pinned her beneath him facedown, his hands beneath her cupping her breasts, his erection furrowing searing undulations between her buttocks.

With gush after gush of readiness flooding her core, she undulated her hips against his hardness in a frenzy, eliciting a rumble of savage triumph from deep in his chest. "*Agápi mou, ne, ne.* Show me. Show me how much you need me."

And she did. She turned her head, blindly reaching for his lips, squirming beneath him, in heat. He caught her lower lip in a growling bite, sucked and pulled on it until it swelled, until she sobbed. Every part of her was disintegrating with the need to take him inside her. He anchored her with a bite where her neck flowed into her shoulder, and slipped one hand beneath her, probing her molten flesh until he took her over the edge. She screamed his name in a soul-searing climax.

As she was still in the throes, and with one hand still stimulating her, he crammed a pillow beneath her hips, spread her wide, then drove his erection all the way inside her drenched, clenching tightness.

Pleasure detonated from every inch of flesh that yielded to his red-hot thickness and length. Unleashed now, he powered into her, growling words of lust in English and Greek as he ravaged her mouth with scorching kisses, while his thrusting manhood drove her to mindlessness.

Ecstasy reverberated inside her with each thrust, each word, like the rushing and receding of a tide gone mad. It all gathered, swelling to its zenith like a tidal wave before the devastating crash.

Before it did, Andreas left her body and swept

her around, his bulk and hands splaying her thighs wide in ferocious urgency.

Then he plunged inside her all the way again, this time finding what he was seeking, the gate to her innermost core, lodging into her womb. "Now, *agápi mou*. Come all over me…*now*."

And she did, the coil of maddening need snapping, lashing through her, over and over again. She screamed, bucked beneath him with each blow of release that pummeled her.

He rode her harder through the storm, causing the shock waves to expand, to raze her, to wring her around his girth in contractions so violent they fractured her breaths, strangled her shrieks. She writhed in an agony of ecstasy, crushed herself against him, around him, inside and out, as if she'd assimilate him and dissolve around him.

In the depths of delirium, she heard him roar his release, felt his seed splash against her over-sensitized flesh, causing another wave to crash down on her, shattering her completely with the brutality of sensations.

It could have been minutes or hours before she lurched back to awareness. She found him spread beneath her, still hard and pulsating inside her, setting off mini quakes that kept her in a state of continuous orgasm.

He was regarding her with the same predatory intensity as before. As soon as she met his eyes he pressed her tight to his length and said, "Call Malcolm and put him out of his misery."

The gruff words interrupted her renewed swooning, made her jerk back. "What?"

Andreas looked positively menacing as he rumbled, "He asked you to marry him, didn't he?"

She pushed against him. "How do you know that?"

He let her put distance between them, reluctantly leaving her body. "He said something when I called him that made me realize he was going to make a move. He made it, didn't he?"

"And I told him it wouldn't work." Her heart started to thud painfully as she struggled to a sitting position. "Does this have anything to do with you hauling me off to your bed, literally? You were making sure I would say no to him?"

Andreas gathered her against his hot, hard body once more, his eyes so possessive she felt he was already invading her again. "I was damned if I was going to take it slow anymore, only for you to settle into considering me a friend, leaving you wide open for another man to make a move on you."

She struggled out of his arms, tumbling deeper into an abyss from the heights, which his possession had catapulted her to. "Well, he made it and I declined, so you didn't have to go to the effort of sabotaging him."

"I would have carried you off to my bed sooner or later. I have him to thank for making it tonight."

"Now you have. Hope you're satisfied."

Andreas trapped her beneath him again, ending her struggle, his eyes crackling with hunger. "I'm nowhere near satisfied. After all this deprivation I'll need a steady and intensive diet of you before I begin to remember what satisfaction feels like."

This felt real. But where had that passion been those forty-one nights he'd counted so accurately?

"I thought you no longer wanted to take me up on my offer."

"Of unlimited sex? I certainly don't. And I don't want to remarry you, either."

The words fell on her heart like a mallet.

She'd already known he didn't. But hearing him say it, and after what had just happened between them…

"I want to *marry* you. The first time doesn't count."

She gaped at him, her heart forgetting to beat.

"I've been trying to prove to you it would work between us this time, that I can be there for you and Dorothea in a family setting. I struggled to keep sex out of it to make it a real test for me, to prove it to myself as much as to you. But I guess we both know now where my limits are."

All this had been a test? He'd been demonstrating to himself before he did to her that he could be a family man?

Apprehension melting, she reached out a trembling hand to smooth the tension from his face. "I wish you had reached your limits way before now. Not that I didn't love exploring other sides to you, finding out about them even as you found them out about yourself."

Anxious eagerness flared in his eyes. "You did?"

She pulled him down, planted a tremulous kiss on that knotted brow. "Oh, I certainly did."

He groaned as his arms tightened around her. "I want you to forget everything that happened between us before."

She pushed away, allowing indulgence to enter her eyes and caress at last. "But there were so many memorable events."

"Toss them out. I'll give you new ones, as frequent as your voluptuous delight of a body can withstand."

That sounded like a dream come true.

Or it would have, if he'd said he loved her.

But he wanted her, and he wanted to give everything to Dora, and to the family they'd form around her. Whether their relationship or his emotions for her ever deepened beyond that, remained to be seen. But Naomi had been ready to settle for far, far less with him.

So she'd be marrying him again knowing she felt more for him than he did for her, but this time she had a hope the emotions he'd spent a lifetime suppressing would blossom enough that he'd love her back one day.

Until then, she'd take whatever she could with him and with Dora, the two pieces that made her heart, and the glue that held together her soul, her world.

He'd started making love to her again, but before he joined them together, he paused above her, tremors of tension traversing his great body as he groaned, "You haven't said yes, *agápi mou.*"

She drew him inside her, gave herself over to him completely and cried out, "Yes, Andreas, *yes.*"

Eleven

Announcing their impending marriage to Hannah and to Andreas's family was more emotional than anything she'd expected. To say everyone was delighted would be the understatement of the decade. But everyone also said they'd been certain this was coming. Seemed they'd all known things only Naomi had been oblivious to.

Then Andreas insisted on having the wedding on Crete, and as soon as possible, setting everything on hyperdrive, with Naomi finding herself in a situation she'd never experienced—becoming part of a large family.

Not that it was only she and Dora who were being engulfed and assimilated into the Sarantos family. Andreas was experiencing his family, whom he'd purposely alienated himself from since childhood, for the first time, too. And it was heart-wrenchingly poignant watching him sinking into their warmth and reciprocating it.

But it was Andreas himself who made her feel giddy with delight and hope for the future. Each day that passed he was becoming the man she'd sensed he could be all these years beneath the reticence and distance. He was opening up to her more every day, making a concerted effort to be there for her in every way. He was going all out to give her everything he hadn't given her in the past, and so many things she hadn't even known to hope for.

They'd arrived in Crete three weeks ago. And this time, Andreas had left it up to her to pick the house that would be their home for when they were in his homeland. He'd insisted she was the one who knew real estate, and that even without her expertise, he would have given her carte blanche to choose whatever house she wanted. He had given her the same with his whole life, anyway.

Though she wasn't about to take advantage of that total offer, she was touched beyond expression that he'd made it. She sometimes wanted to tell him to take it easy on her. It wasn't advisable to make her love him more than she already did.

But she'd eagerly taken him up on his offer to pick their home. There'd been one specific villa she'd dreamed of sharing with him from the moment she'd seen it.

It was in the Réthymno region, Crete's smallest prefecture. It was an area synonymous with gorgeous mountainscapes and beaches, legendary caves, historic monasteries and monuments, traditional mountain villages and luxurious holiday resorts. She'd been captured by the essence of mythical Crete in this remote and self-sufficient region from the first time she'd set foot in it.

The villa, which had felt like home the first time Andreas had set foot in it with her, was dominated at its back by the Lefká Ori, what the impressive White Mountains were called locally. Overlooking the crystalline waters of the Sea of Crete, it was nestled on a glorious stretch of white-gold beach. It was big enough to accommodate all the family who would come visiting, yet secluded enough for the two of them to forget an outside world existed.

And today, an hour from now, at the magical sunset hour, they would have their wedding there.

It would be nothing elaborate, since they couldn't

even think of it with their recent losses. Just a relatively small ceremony with their family and close friends present, where they'd exchange their vows. Their first vows.

"You better be ready." Caliope walked into the room where Naomi was dressing. Andreas's sister was starting to waddle in her eighth month, her turquoise chiffon bridesmaid dress reflecting the color of her eyes and the waters surrounding the villa.

Accompanying her, Selene smirked at Naomi as she helped Caliope into a seat. She was wearing a similar dress, albeit one that hugged her trim figure.

"Andreas seems about to start tossing everyone in that gorgeous infinity pool you're having the ceremony around," Selene explained.

Naomi blinked, her heart starting to hammer. "Why? What's wrong?"

Caliope chuckled. "You don't get that you've unleashed the volcano that seethed beneath the ice, do you? The man is sizzling to make you his wife again…or for real, according to him. Aristedes sent us to fetch you ahead of time, as Andreas is working himself into a lather with all sorts of anxieties."

Her gut knotted. "What anxieties?"

Selene waved dismissively. "Just those that plague every breath of those who love too much."

Caliope and Selene thought Andreas loved her? Like their men loved them? It was so easy to think he did, with everything he did for her. Not that he'd said the words.

But she didn't need those anymore. She had far more than she'd ever dreamed she would. And it was all because of him.

She took one last look at herself in the mirror, her heart turning in her chest at the sight of the radiant bride looking back at her. Andreas had gotten her the most luxurious wedding gown she'd ever laid eyes on, a dream of snow-white chiffon, satin and lace that hugged her figure, ripened her every curve. Every cultural influence that made up Crete was represented in its materials, cut and embellishments. The gown made her feel like the heroine of an ancient Greek fairy tale, a mortal about to join her life with the god who'd chosen her for his mate.

Caliope sighed. "You look beyond perfect, Naomi, a golden goddess, like Andreas always calls you."

Selene chuckled, then she echoed what Naomi

had just thought. "Now hurry before your mate's wrath befalls the mere mortals awaiting your celestial ceremony."

A giggle overpowered Naomi as she gathered her courage and ran out, feeling she was rushing to meet her destiny.

As she walked through the open, sun-drenched spaces of their new home, their trio was joined by the other bridesmaids—all of Andreas's sisters and oldest nieces, and Hannah's three daughters and her oldest granddaughters. Hannah herself was waiting for them outside with Dora.

With every step, it felt as if Naomi was forging deeper into a tranquil paradise. Her bridal procession stepped out onto the elevated open-air deck leading to the infinity pool, its glittering aquamarine waters segueing seamlessly into those of the sea. The sun was turning flame-orange and speeding on an intercept course with the horizon.

The combination of such pristine nature and lavish human design was breathtaking. When they were alone here, it felt as if they were the only man and woman on earth.

Right now, dozens of people were around, all dressed in colors complementing the setting, their faces painted in smiles. But Naomi could barely feel their presence. There was only one person in her awareness. Andreas. The man she'd loved from the first moment and would love till her last breath.

With his collar-length hair blowing in the balmy breeze, every strand reflecting a different hue of the sun, he wore a white-on-white suit with an open-necked shirt and a gold rose in his lapel. He stood there, waiting to be one with her, in a pristine new beginning, every inch the Greek god that had come down to earth to choose a mortal for his bride. Naomi could only wonder again how it could possibly be her.

He suddenly broke away from the group of men he stood among—Aristedes, her partners and Selene's brothers—and strode toward her in an unrehearsed move. Naomi found herself breaking from her own companions and running to meet him halfway. Then she was in his strong arms, swept up and whirled around and around.

Laughing, tears flowing, she clung to his neck as he carried her back to the priest, who was in full Cretan garb. The ceremony, in both English and Greek, began with Andreas clasping her to his heart. She couldn't have dreamed of a better place to be for these life-changing moments.

As soon as they'd exchanged their rings and

vows, and before the priest instructed him to kiss the bride, Andreas was devouring her and she was giving in to his passion, just as she'd so long ago surrendered all of her heart and soul to him.

Suddenly, something pulled her out of the dream world of his possession. Cries of surprise, ones she doubted were in response to his passionate display.

Andreas raised his head, too, and they both turned to the source of the excitement. It was Dora. Standing in front of Hannah, whose face was streaming in tears.

Dora was *standing*.

Then she took her first step.

In unspoken agreement, Naomi and Andreas ran toward her, both going down on their knees, their arms outstretched, their voices raised in ragged encouragement, for her to come bless their new union and complete the circle of their newly forged family.

To the thunderous cheering of all present, the determined darling—Nadine's and Petros's baby, and now hers and Andreas's in every way—kept going, putting one chubby leg unsteadily in front of the other, until she reached them and threw herself into Andreas's arms with a piercing squeal of triumph.

Then Naomi found Dora in her arms and both of them in Andreas's embrace, kissed and cosseted and claimed.

Naomi clung to Dora, to Andreas, wept with joy and prayed that she'd always be blessed with both of them, to love and to live for, for the rest of her life.

"This is not a Cretan wedding ritual...it's a cretin one."

Andreas's growl was met by generalized laughter, from his brother and the few guests who remained after the reception. He deeply regretted succumbing to the custom of keeping the groom away from the bride while she "prepared" herself for him.

He'd thought it would be a few minutes when he'd agreed to the harebrained idea. Aristedes had just informed him it would be one more hour.

Then his brother had the temerity to add, "Waiting will only intensify your desire. And besides, we haven't gotten a chance to exchange two sentences in the last several weeks."

"And you think the time to rectify that is on my wedding night? Are you nuts, Aristedes?" Andreas glared at him, then at Selene's brothers, the Louvardis trio who'd been ribbing the hell out of him in their oblivious bachelordom.

He heaved up to his feet, and they all followed suit, to try to make him sit down.

"Stand aside, all of you, and no one needs to get hurt."

More laughter met his threat, with everyone teasing him about his eagerness.

If only they knew he wasn't joking.

If he didn't get to Naomi at once, it might turn ugly.

After a lifetime of total control, ever since everything inside him had been unleashed, he no longer knew the man that had emerged from that self-imposed prison. He was still getting to know this new being, tentatively testing his triggers, and wary about provoking his boundless emotions and bottomless needs. And those had been dangerously provoked since he'd last seen Naomi.

It was unreasoning, the panic he felt every time she was out of his sight now. What he felt for her, and for Dorothea, was so acute at times, so agonizing, he sometimes wished for the days when everything inside him had been under airtight containment, and he could control how much he let out. He now knew the difference between his obsession with Naomi when his emotions had been stifled, and now, when nothing was held back anymore.

Now he left his companions behind and homed in on her vibe through this house that had already become his home, because she'd chosen it, because she and Dorothea were in it.

He burst into their room, found her lying on her side on the bed, an arm thrown over one of the bouquets he'd flooded the whole house with. She lurched around, her gaze as feverish as he knew his must be. So it was the same with her, as if they'd been breathing barely enough oxygen to survive. Now they got to gulp down all they needed to live, to soar.

He came down on his knees at the foot of the bed. Her smooth legs, which had grown honey-tanned under his agonized eyes these last weeks, were exposed as the traditional Cretan white wedding gown that made her look like an angel and a goddess in one rode up to her thighs.

The beast roaring inside him wanted to drag her, slam her into his flesh, overpower and invade and brand her.

And he'd done that, so many times before, to their mutual explosive ecstasy. But now…now it was different. Now they'd entered a new realm. He wanted to show her all the special things she'd unearthed inside him. He wanted to cherish her.

She gasped as he slipped her shoes off, and tried to turn to him fully. He stopped her with a gentle hand at the small of her back. She subsided with a whimpering exhalation, watched him with her plump bottom lip caught in her white teeth as he prowled forward on all fours, advancing over her, kissing and suckling his way from the soles of her feet, up her legs, her thighs, her buttocks and back, her nape. All the while, he unraveled ribbons, undid hooks and caressed the dress off her mind-blowing body. She lay beneath him, quaking and moaning at each touch, until he traced the lines of her shuddering profile with his lips. The moment he reached her mouth, she cried out, twisted on her back, surged up to cling to his lips in a desperate, soul-wrenching kiss.

Lowering her to the bed, he pulled back to take in her nakedness. No fantasy had conjured the beauty that had held his libido hostage from their first time together.

"*Monadíkos, agápi mou*...unique."

And she was. Her beauty eclipsed that of the

hundreds of white, cream and gold roses he'd filled their bedroom with.

Needing to worship her, to curb his hunger, tame it into tenderness, he found his hands were shaking as he undressed under her wide-eyed gaze and breathless encouragement.

Then he was all over her again, tracing the satin of her skin from toes to cheeks, tasting and kneading and nibbling, strumming every tremor out of her body.

Finally rising above her, he reveled in the sight, scent and sounds of her surrender, every shudder and moan pulverizing his intentions to be infinitely slow and gentle. Blood thundered in his head, in his loins, tearing the tatters of control from his grasp in a riptide.

Then she took it all out of his hands, hers sweeping over his back and buttocks in silent demand, their power absolute.

He surrendered, came between her shaking thighs, pressed her shuddering breasts beneath his aching chest. Then she conquered him, irrevocably.

Against his forehead, her lips prayed a litany of his name, and she clasped him to her body as if she couldn't believe he was there. Poignancy swamped him, choked him. He had to prove to her that he would always be there, was hers forever.

He rose on his knees, cupped her head, her buttocks, tilted one for his kiss, the other for his penetration. He bathed the head of his erection in the hot, moist silk of her luxurious welcome, absorbed her cries of pleasure, drinking in her pleas to take her, fill her.

Succumbed to the mercilessness of their need, he drew back to watch her eyes as he started to sink into her. Her flesh fluttered around his advance, hot and tight almost beyond endurance.

Her fingers dug into his shoulders, forcing him to stroke deeper into her. She cried out, a sharp sound of exultation that tore a growl of pride out of him.

She never took her eyes off his, letting him see every sensation ripping through her, her honeyed complexion brightening with her rising pleasure, burning up the dark gold she lay on.

"*Panémorfi*...gorgeous beyond description *agápi mou*," he said, his voice a ragged rasp. "The masters would have paid in blood to capture your beauty for eternity. And the way you feel inside... madness, magnificence."

She sobbed, thrashed her head, her hair rioting

around her shoulders, a thousand shades of gold gleaming against the dark sheets. "It's you who's beautiful beyond words...you who feels magnificent...inside me. Give me all of you, *agápi mou.* Take all of me...."

Hearing the Greek words trembling on her lips was such a surprise, he almost keeled over her. She'd never said "my love" to him in any language.

He rose on extended arms, surveyed her feverishly. He'd always known there'd been need on her side. But without the trust, the certainty, he'd known that love hadn't been possible, not the way he'd seen it with his siblings. Was Naomi developing a new dimension to her emotions? Or was this endearment only fueled by pleasure and the maddening need for release?

Not that it mattered. She'd pledged to be with him, let him be with her and Dorothea, forever. He'd take what she could give when she could give it. Need could become love.

Now she needed fulfillment. And he'd give her all she could ever need.

Feeding her hunger for more of him, he thrust deeply inside her, watching in receding sanity as she accepted all of him, wild, abandoned. Then she was weeping as she sought his lips, her mouth and tongue dueling with his as her core throbbed around his invasion, demanding he take her harder, faster. He had to obey her.

His rhythm quickened. Plunging became pounding until her cries rose to a shriek that ripped through him. She arched up, coming around him in a climax so intense it shredded her screams, wrenched at his shaft. The knowledge that he was fulfilling her tore his own release from his recesses.

With a prayer that his seed would one day take root in her womb and create a miracle like Dorothea, he jetted inside her, prolonging her orgasm. One detonation after another of ecstasy rocked him, and her, locked them in a closed circuit of over-stimulation, dissolved them into one.

When it felt as if his heart would never restart, the tumult gave way to the warmth and weakness of satiation. He felt her melt beneath him, satisfaction and awe glowing on her face.

"*Ómorfi gynaíka mou,*" he rumbled as he twisted, bringing her on top while maintaining their merging.

She opened her lips over his heart. What she said almost ripped it out of his ribs. "*Ómorfi sýzygó mou.*"

He lurched with surprise, squeezed her tighter to him. "You understood."

She nodded, planting kisses all over his chest. "I know more Greek than you realize."

He raised her head, gazed into her heavenly, drugged with pleasure eyes, his heart booming. That she'd learned Greek, no doubt for him, at least enough to understand his words, that she'd answered his proclamation, calling him her beautiful husband, had delight bursting inside him. Resurging desire, too, since she'd purred the words in that new voice she now used with him, breathless, aware, overcome.

She rose a bit, her hair draping over his chest like a sheath of spun gold. She gave him such a smile, no inhibitions, satiated, yet insatiable. "Now that you've given me tenderness, it's time you ravaged me."

He crushed her to him, hunger raging again as if he hadn't just found total satisfaction inside her. "Your wish is my command, always. You can consider this just the appetizer, to get you ready for the main courses I have planned for the rest of the night."

"Oh, yes, yes, please…" she moaned her eager surrender, her face blazing at his promise, her body blossoming under his, undulating in a renewed dance of sinuous demand and submission.

"I will please you. I live to please and pleasure you." Gathering her in his arms, he rose from the bed.

Then with her clasped to his heart he walked out through the now deserted house to the pool where they'd joined their lives. All the way there, she caressed and kissed him, clung to him as if she was a part of him.

And for the rest of the night, he took her, gave himself to her, with every exercise of possession and ecstasy deepening her sensual enslavement. And his.

It was dawn by the time Andreas had finished fulfilling his pledge, giving Naomi a wedding night that had surpassed even their most explosive times together. Every touch, every breath, had been pure ecstasy.

Now she lay nestled against his side, knowing for the first time what perfection felt like.

But was it possible for everything to be so perfect?

And remain so?

Life had taught her that any measure of happiness had to exact a terrible price.

What would be the price of all this bliss? And when would fate demand its payment?

Twelve

Waking up in bed with Andreas, after making love deep into the night, and lying there with him, entwined, savoring the echoes of passion, building up to another plunge, all the while *talking,* had became Naomi's new addiction.

But that was only one of the delights that abounded in their lives now. A favorite one was not remembering where they were when she opened her eyes every morning, what with the way they commuted between Crete and New York.

It kept everything breathlessly exciting and was the best of all possible worlds. And as if they'd always done this, they'd thrown themselves into their shared life, mixing being passionate newlyweds with being Dora's parents, and active members of "their" family with running their businesses. Keeping that exhilarating balance was possible only because of the other's input and support. At least Naomi hoped she was as vital in making all that possible for Andreas as he was for her.

He did insist that he was discovering himself right along with her, and that the discoveries were all thanks to her. She truly hoped she was helping him mine the treasures inside him. She had no doubt she'd keep finding more in his depths, and more reasons to love him. She now believed all the heartache had been a tiny price for the privilege of finding him, of recognizing his truth even against all evidence, and of ending up having what she now had with him.

He raised his head from nuzzling her neck, running a hand heavy with possession and satisfaction down her back, his eyes eloquent with both as they met hers.

They'd been talking about Dora's first birthday party and how wonderfully everything had come together, and jokingly planning her second one. Or at least Naomi had been joking. She wouldn't put it past him to be talking seriously.

He sighed with pleasure as he sifted his fingers

through her hair. "But I guess we can't make solid plans now, since by the time she's two, she'll probably have her own demands for her party."

Naomi chuckled. "I was right! You *were* serious!"

He squeezed her to his length, his leg driving in sensuous playfulness between hers. "Yes, laugh at the man who's been hurled from one extreme to the other."

Her hands luxuriated in the depths of his hair, just as her legs did in rubbing his between them. "I only do since you seem to enjoy the excruciating change so much."

"And how. And excruciating change is right." As he rose up on one elbow, a serious cast came over his face. "I still remember exactly how it felt at the time, yet I can't believe I ever feared having a child."

Her heart convulsed at the memory of the confrontation that had ended her hope of being with him in the past.

She ran her hand down his hard cheek, wanting to absorb any recriminations he might have. "That fear was just you being responsible, when you suspected you might have inherited your father's coldheartedness. Though if you didn't have I

Kyría's ax hanging over your head, that fear should have made you realize you were nothing like him. Callous people don't fear their potential damage to others."

"I wasn't about to test whether I would turn out to be my father or not, not with a child's life on the line." Andreas shook his head, as if in wonderment. "Then fate delivered me Dorothea."

The magnitude of emotion he transmitted in those words felt like an earthquake shaking through Naomi.

She took refuge in voicing something she'd been wondering about. "You never call her Dora."

His lips melted with the profound fondness he reserved only for Dora. "It's the way I've thought of her from the first moment. That little magical creature from a realm I never dreamed I could enter." Suddenly, he frowned, as if hit by an idea he'd never considered. "But I'll call her Dora if you prefer."

Naomi cupped his face in urgent hands, wiping away the frown. "Oh, no, I actually love it that you have your own name for her. I think she knows it, too, and it's part of the special bond that has developed between you. Something that's only yours and no one else's, not even mine."

"I hope you're right, on her side. On mine, something inexplicable happened inside me from the first moment I saw her. Even when I was unequipped at the time to realize what it was. Everything that Petros meant to me was mingled with her own delightful cuteness and the way she reached out to me with her curiosity and acceptance. I think she instinctively recognized my involvement and just went ahead and claimed me. I felt overwhelmed by the need to protect her, but my fear of myself was so long entrenched I couldn't trust what I was experiencing, and I had to be certain it was real."

"It didn't take you long to become certain."

"I was irrevocably involved after that first evening, then the first day in our Manhattan Beach house. But I was still not certain how I'd react in the long run, on a constant basis, if she became a major part of my daily life. But after that month, I became certain. What I felt from the start was real, and it will only become more profound with time. There is absolutely nothing I wouldn't do for her, and I can't imagine I could ever love anything as much as I love our precious Dorothea."

Not even a child of our own?

It had been too soon to bring up even the idea

of one, with everything they'd had to achieve during the last two months to create their shared life. Naomi had inserted an IUD the day after she'd gone to his suite and had intended to keep it in place until they made a decision when to have more babies. She'd had no doubt their time would come.

But now doubts were insidiously creeping in. What if Andreas wanted Dora because she'd already existed? What if she was so special to him he wouldn't want another child?

Naomi debated whether to vocalize her worries. Then he started to make love to her again and every mental process stopped, his passion and the pleasure he gave her short-circuiting them.

But afterward, when she was outside his field of influence, doubts returned with a vengeance.

She was beyond delighted that he loved Dora as if she was his own. Delighted for him and for Dora. But knowing that he'd felt that fiercely for Dora from the beginning unsettled her. It took her back to thinking she'd been incidental to all this. Especially since there was one more thing she couldn't escape. That he hadn't been anywhere near this vocal about how he felt for *her*.

What if he was this wonderful to her only because of his determination to give Dora the best life? What if all his actions were fueled by the bottomless paternal reserves he'd discovered within himself?

But even if that was true, what could she do about it? She had entered this marriage, again, knowing she felt more for him than he'd ever feel for her.

"Stop it."

She had to hiss the self-admonition out loud to abort the spiral of malignant thoughts.

She *wouldn't* fret and invent heartaches. She *would* be endlessly grateful for the blessing of having him and Dora in her life.

Two weeks later, they were back in New York, and she'd been clinging to her decision, had been letting their full lives together sweep her on an unstoppable tide.

But in spite of all her efforts, vague dreads weighed down her every waking and sleeping moment. Until the worst of it had manifested last night.

Andreas had had to shake her awake, to drag her from the depths of a nightmare where he and Dora had kept receding, with her running and screaming after them, until they disappeared.

By the time he'd managed to snatch her from the dream's tentacles, she'd been sobbing and shaking, had remained inconsolable in spite of all his efforts to soothe her. She hadn't told him what she'd dreamed about.

For it hadn't felt like a dream, but a premonition.

He'd refused to leave her to go to work, until she'd told him she was going out herself. When he'd insisted on accompanying her, she'd assured him that an ob-gyn office wasn't the place for him. Still, she'd had to pretend she was fully over her night terror, and swear her doctor visit was only a checkup, before Andreas had relented. Nevertheless, he'd promised he'd be home when she returned.

She'd always had difficult periods when she was troubled. But after she'd given birth to Dora, things had become so much better. Until lately. It had to be something *that* unbearable for her to go to Dr. Summers. Naomi didn't want to see the woman—Nadine's obstetrician and also hers during her pregnancy—for all the memories she'd bring back. She had even gone to a different doctor for her IUD. Now she was wondering if the device was behind her unusually painful period, forcing her to seek the expertise of the doctor who knew her and her history.

An hour later, Miriam Summers grinned at her after she concluded her exam and drew some blood for tests.

"Everything is in order, with the IUD at least."

Jumping up to adjust her clothes, Naomi followed her out to her office. "At least? What else isn't in order?"

The woman waved. "Nothing, really. You just have congestion in the pelvic area, and I think this is what's causing the pain and heaviness."

"Could it be psychological?"

Miriam chuckled. "Actually, it's very physiological. It's a classic sign of sustained and unrelieved arousal. You and your husband don't have to abstain from sex in all forms while you have your period, you know."

"Oh. *Oh.*"

Andreas had been all for alternative methods, but it had been she who'd refused, afraid it might be unappealing for him.

At her silence, Miriam rushed to add, "I haven't seen you or Nadine since Dora was born, so I have no idea what's been going on with your lives. I mentioned a husband because I noticed the wedding band, and I hope I wasn't out of line."

Naomi stared at her. How could she have forgotten this? Miriam Summers had no idea her sister was dead.

The woman groaned. "Seems every time I open my mouth I make it worse. What did I say wrong now?"

"Nothing, nothing..." Then, after taking a moment to collect herself, she told her about Nadine.

The doctor was evidently shocked. The silence that reigned over her elegant office became more oppressive by the second.

Then Miriam spoke again, hushed and heavy. "I can't tell you how terribly sorry I am, Naomi. Nadine was one of my favorite patients, and it isn't every day I see a relationship like the one you two had. I am so sorry for your loss, but..."

She stopped, seemed to be struggling with something huge.

"But...but what, Doctor?"

"I think now that both Nadine and Petros are dead, you should know the truth."

The truth.
The truth. *The truth.*

The words reverberated inside Naomi's head as she walked New York's streets aimlessly.

The truth about Dora. And about Nadine.

Nadine had had no viable eggs. But Petros had loved her too much, had known how bereft she'd feel if she couldn't have that child she'd wanted more than anything in life. He'd begged Dr. Summers not to tell her about her total infertility, but to find an egg donor and let Nadine think the baby was hers.

Dora wasn't what remained to Naomi of Nadine. Wasn't related to her in any way.

What would happen when Andreas realized she had no claim to Dora, the baby who'd become the daughter he loved above all else, when he'd never once intimated he might want another one with her?

Then, as always when suspicions started, they spiraled from terrible to insupportable.

Maybe he'd known all along. Maybe he was now adopting Dora, but wouldn't make Naomi her mother officially. Maybe he wouldn't so it would be mess-free when he eventually had enough of her, and she eventually exited their lives. Maybe he'd only needed her because she'd been his path to Dora, married her because he wasn't certain

Dora would grow attached to him without her help, without the security of her presence, and in the normalcy of a family life that only marriage could provide. But Dora was now more attached to him than to Naomi. Maybe now her use to him was over.

Logic said that if Andreas intended to end her presence in Dora's life one day, he'd do it while she was young enough to forget Naomi without repercussions to her psyche. Like she had forgotten Nadine and Petros as if they'd never been.

Now Naomi could see only two possibilities.

Either Andreas didn't know, and when he did, he'd still want to include her in their lives forever, if only for Dora's sake. Or the worst scenario was true, and she'd exit their lives in the not too distant future. She had no reason to think there'd be a third possibility.

Andreas didn't love her.

In his new vocal emotionalism, he would have said something if he did.

But he hadn't.

Somehow, she made her way to the house that no longer felt like home. Entering it, she felt as she had the first time she'd come here, like a guest reluctantly stepping into a place where she didn't belong, and might never return.

His presence deluged her even before she saw him exiting his study and striding toward her, his expression anxious.

He caught her to him, swept her off the ground in a tight embrace, before withdrawing to bestow kisses all over her face. "I was just about to go out looking for you!"

She forced her limbs to remain steady as she pushed out of his arms. She'd lived with uncertainty for far too long. Now all she needed was to know. Once and for all.

He was reaching for her again when she stopped him. By two words. *"I know."*

If she'd had any doubts, they evaporated in the heat of what flared in his eyes. Admission.

He'd known, too. All along.

Her nightmare, her premonition was coming true.

Both he and Dora had never belonged to her, but now belonged together. They would need her less every day, would recede until they vanished completely.

And she couldn't wait for this to happen slowly.

If she was to die, she'd rather it was in one brutal blow.

"Naomi…"

She talked over him, her voice that of a drone. "Now that I know I am not related to Dora, I realize why Petros didn't even mention me in his will. He only wanted me to take care of his daughter until you stepped in. And now you have, and my role in her life is over."

"How can you say that? Dorothea needs you. She—"

Naomi again interrupted. "I know you'd go to any lengths to give her everything you think she needs. But she now has you. She loves you, and she'll forget me in no time once I'm gone."

"*Theos*, Naomi, *ne…*"

"I will tell Hannah everything, ask her to stay on with you if you want her. Then I will leave. This time, don't draw things out thinking I'll change my mind. I won't."

Andreas watched Naomi walk away, déjà vu pummeling him.

But it didn't feel like the past all over again. It felt a thousand times worse.

When she'd walked away before she'd looked wrecked. This time she looked…cold. As if there was nothing left inside her. As if the moment she'd found out that Dorothea wasn't her sister's child, she'd stopped caring. About her...and about him.

This was like nothing he'd feared when he'd hidden the truth from her from the start.

He'd been unable to take away her comfort in believing she had a physical part of her sister still alive and growing under her eyes and in her arms. The baby she considered her daughter, having given birth to her, and having raised her with her sister, then alone.

But was it possible she didn't love Dorothea as if she was her own? That all her feelings toward her had only been an extension of her love for Nadine, and therefore gone the moment that connection was shattered in her mind?

And what about him? He'd thought she...felt something real and intense for him. He'd thought she'd come to depend on him as he'd come to depend on her for his very breath.

Had he been mistaken, too, about what they shared?

He wanted to storm after her, tell her he wasn't letting her go this time. But how could he hope to keep her, if she didn't love Dorothea?

If she'd never loved him?

* * *

"Are you sure this is about what it seems to be about?"

Andreas stared at Aristedes. Nothing his brother or Caliope had said in so far had made any sense.

In an unprecedented approach, knowing true desperation for the first time in his life, Andreas had reached out for their counsel, before he lost his mind irrevocably.

After he'd told them the little he knew, they'd asked him a hundred questions. This last one didn't make more sense than any before it.

"What I mean is," Aristedes elaborated, "Are you sure this is about Dora? As big a shock as it is for Naomi to discover the child isn't Nadine's biologically, I don't see how it would cause such a drastic reaction on its own."

Caliope nodded. "Knowing what I know about Naomi, this sounds like it was the last straw."

"What last straw?" Andreas barked, his nerves snapping. "Everything was perfect. Up till…"

He suddenly remembered that nightmare she'd had. Those terrible moments she'd writhed in his arms in her sleep, and wept in such agony and desperation.

He related the incident, which had shaken him

to his core, and which had only been eclipsed by the much bigger blow of what had happened a few hours later.

"But that was a nightmare! It couldn't have anything to do with what happened."

Caliope pursed her lips. "Maybe it wasn't a nightmare but a manifestation of all her fears and doubts and uncertainties from the past. They might have never been resolved, and they got the best of her while she slept."

"You mean her past with me? But the past has nothing to do with the present. I was a different man then. Or…do you mean that whatever emotional injury I caused her in the past has never healed, and it's why she couldn't love me now?"

Aristedes shook his head. "From what she told me, and from what I observed of her with you, I believe the past is to blame, but not in the way you think. It's actually because you didn't really change your ways in the present."

"What *are* you talking about? She was just telling me how I've changed from one extreme to the other."

"You have, where reaching out and taking what you need from others is concerned. But what about reaching out with your emotions? Have you told her how you feel about her? *Do* you feel anything for *her*, Naomi herself, beyond her being the third piece in this family unit you've become so dependent on and believe you can't live without?"

"So you think I turned from being passively self-centered and self-serving to actively, aggressively so?" Andreas seethed. "I had feelings for only her, even when I thought I had none. I always loved her, and now I do more than I thought possible. I worship her and I certainly can't live without her. As *her* and her alone."

Aristedes and Caliope exchanged a patient glance that had him on the verge of tearing the place down.

Before he did, Aristedes turned to him. "Have you told *her* that?"

"Of course I—"

He stopped abruptly, the breath knocked out of him at the enormity of the realization.

He hadn't.

His head spinning, he choked out, "I kept showing her…" He stopped, his protest clogging in his throat.

"You mean you never made a declaration like the one you just made to us?" Caliope prodded.

He squeezed his eyes shut. "No."

"Not once? Nothing close? In the past or now?"

He could only shake his head, feeling as if he was suffocating.

Caliope squared her shoulders. "Okay then, here's what I think she thinks, what led to what she did today. She always loved you, but you never reciprocated, beyond physically. Then you came back, but the only emotional involvement you exhibited was with Dora. Naomi thinks that you married her to provide Dora with a family. From her viewpoint, you never loved her, and whatever you think you've been doing to demonstrate your love hasn't shown her you love her for herself. The longer you made no emotional declaration to her personally, the more it left her feeling unvalued and unloved, and worst of all, convenient. With the blow of finding out she had no claim to Dora, she must be feeling unneeded, too, totally cut adrift. Once she believed her main value to you is convenience, it was only one step further to think it would one day end. By walking away now, she's saving herself more pain later on, and saving Dora an eventual injury, too."

This all sounded plausible, if only because every word cut him down to his recesses. He'd been so involved in his plans, in showing Naomi his feelings in his own way, he hadn't stopped to think if it was a way she'd understand.

But there was one reality he had to face now. Why he hadn't made an unequivocal confession of his feelings.

He'd felt it would be the ultimate vulnerability. That after he'd said the words, he'd lose his power totally, expose his every weakness. Life had taught him never to do that. And because he'd withheld that last bit of trust from her, he'd lost her.

He grabbed his hair in vicious hands, his groan wrenched from his gut. "I can't lose her. I *can't*."

Caliope rushed to put her arm around him. "You don't have to. Just go tell her what you just told us."

"The time for words is past, Caliope." Aristedes shook his head, his eyes solemn as he met his. "Naomi loves you with every fiber of her being, Andreas. It killed her, being with you in the past while she thought you didn't share that same depth of involvement. It remains her doubt and heartache now. It was why she left you once, and why she left you again. All she ever wanted was your love. If you can't *prove* that she has it, has always had it, that you would love her forever, no matter what, and above everything and *everyone*...then you *will* lose her."

* * *

Next morning, Andreas was standing in front of Naomi's apartment, bracing for another struggle.

She made it all unnecessary when she opened the door.

The moment he saw her he knew that every word Aristedes and Caliope had said was true. Naomi loved him with everything in her. It was why she looked as if everything in her had been extinguished.

Instead of such love being in his favor, it might be why he wouldn't be able to win her back. This time, she had to have absolute certainty of the depth of his equal emotions. If the evidence he'd brought wasn't enough…

No. He wouldn't consider that possibility.

Though everything in him clamored for her, he had to give her all he had first, before he could hope she'd reclaim him.

Brushing past her, he closed the door behind him, then turned to her. "Do you believe that I love Dorothea, Naomi?"

After a moment of apparent surprise, she nodded. "I do. I think your feelings are even more intense because they came after a lifetime of holding back."

"You already believe I'd do anything for her. But do you realize I'd rather die than give her up?"

Her face seized, her throat worked. She nodded again.

And he presented her with the papers. "This revokes any right I have to Dorothea in your favor. You can now apply to become her sole parent."

Silence. Nothing but silence as she stared at the papers in her hands, then up at him.

"This is my proof to you, *agápi mou,* that Dorothea has nothing to do with us, with why I wanted to marry you. You know I wanted you from the first moment I laid eyes on you, but what you don't know, what I never told you, is that I loved you just as long. I have never been able to articulate my emotions, have even been scared to. I thought it was safer for me to show you, and I've been trying to since I came back. I have so much to learn about how to express my love for you, since it's so huge, so encompassing, I get lost inside it. Though I suspect nothing I could do would ever convey the magnitude of what I feel for you. You are everything to me, Naomi, and I have no life without you."

When she continued to stare at him, her astonishment total, a terrible doubt hit him. "Wasn't that why you left? Because you suspected my motives for being with you? Or did you leave because you no longer love me? Have I killed your feelings for me? Or did you never love me...?"

He suddenly found himself wrapped in her arms so tight his choking breath left him completely. His agitated lips were stilled beneath her trembling ones, tears wetting them, though he didn't know whether they came from his eyes or hers or both.

She studded his face with kisses as she clung harder and harder to him. "I've always, always loved you and will always, always love you. Oh, Andreas, my darling, *s'agapo*..."

Before tension could turn to elation, it resurged on one more paramount dread. "What about Dorothea?"

Naomi withdrew, her face gripped in remembered pain as tears rained down her cheeks. "It almost killed me to walk away from her. But I thought I'd have to give her up one day, and it was better for her if I did it now rather than later."

Andreas crushed Naomi in arms that trembled with too much love, relief and gratitude. "And now, *agápi mou*? Will you take us both back? Will you let me worship you for the rest of my days? Will you be my wife and my lover, the owner of my heart and life? Will you be Dorothea's mother and the pillar of her existence? This precious baby who was made by Petros and Nadine's love, and given life by yours, and will now grow up among us, and among our family, and be treasured for the rest of our lives?"

And he received her answering pledge, which she gave with the whole of her body and soul, giving him all of herself for his safekeeping.

He wallowed in her kisses and confessions, feeling blessed beyond measure. "Naomi, *s'agapo*, I love you, love you so…"

Her phone rang somewhere deep in her apartment. They ignored it. For the first three times. Then, suddenly, they were both running for it, struck by the same fear at once. It could be Hannah…Dora…

It wasn't. From what Naomi said as she answered, Andreas realized it was a doctor. The one she'd gone to see yesterday?

As she listened to the person on the other end, Naomi's face went slack, then she swayed.

Cursing, his fright soaring, Andreas swept her up in his arms as she ended the call, took her to the couch and knelt on the floor before her, grasping her hands. "What is it, *agápi mou?*"

"I—I went in for an exam, and…and…" She drew in a huge breath. "I'm pregnant."

It was his turn to stare. And stare.

Then he exclaimed, "But you had your period!"

She was almost panting now. "It's a false period. It happens. Especially since I have an IUD. The doctor missed it because it is so early, no more than two weeks, but the blood work was conclusive."

Naomi gulped down a breath as she stopped, looking stunned, and something else. Worried?

He squeezed her hands as they shook in his. "Are you worried? About having another baby so soon?"

She shook her head. "Actually, it's about you. You love Dora so much, I was wondering if you could want another—"

His lips stopped her trembling words in a feverish kiss. "I want, Naomi, I *want*. I want another baby made of our love. I want two or three or as many as you want and can have. I want anything and everything…with you."

Withdrawing to read the absolute truth of his words in his eyes, she cried a sound of such relief and delight as she surged to bury her streaming face in his chest.

Then she raised adoring, tear-filled eyes to his.

"And I want anything and everything with you, my love, for the rest of my life."

As tears he'd never known surged from his soul, he pledged to her, "Never again will I let you feel alone, or be without me or without my love. I will spend my life showing you how you reanimated my heart and gave me everything worth living for, how you blessed my life, and saved it."

* * * * *